VILLA FONTAINE

Recent Titles by Julie Ellis from Severn House

AVENGED

DEADLY OBSESSION

GENEVA RENDEZVOUS

THE ITALIAN AFFAIR

NINE DAYS TO KILL

NO GREATER LOVE

SECOND TIME AROUND

VANISHED

WHEN THE SUMMER PEOPLE HAVE GONE

VILLA FONTAINE

Julie Ellis

severn House

This title first published in Great Britain 1999 by
SEVERN HOUSE PUBLISHERS LTD of
9–15 High Street, Sutton, Surrey SM1 1DF.
This title first published in the U.S.A. 1999 by
SEVERN HOUSE PUBLISHERS INC of
595 Madison Avenue, New York, N.Y. 10022.

British Library Cataloguing in Publication Data
Ellis, Julie, 1933-
    Villa Fontaine
        1.   Romantic suspense novels
        I.   Title
        813.5'4 [F]

    ISBN 0 7278 2216 0

Printed and bound in Great Britain by
MPG Books Ltd, Bodmin, Cornwall.

For

Jackie Barr

CHAPTER ONE

The morning was muggy, threatening to break heat records. The Manhattan sky was grey. I stood at the picture window in my so-called luxury studio apartment high over Third Avenue, relishing the air conditioning, and contemplated my projected "fourteen glorious days in London and Paris."

The trip was an extravagance, considering I'd been teaching for only one full year. I assuaged my guilt with the reminder that this was in the nature of an educational expense, since I teach French in a Bronx junior high. Also, the trip would give me a chance to see my gorgeous, effervescent sister Holly, who had been in Rome for almost five months playing small parts in several American films being shot over there. Holly planned to fly to Paris to spend a weekend with me. We'd never been separated so long before.

From the window I spied our postman, who has something like Holly's zest for living. Freddie was walking, with small paper bag in hand, into our building, where the tall sacks of mail waited for distribution.

Give Freddie ten minutes to drink his coffee, to begin sorting the mail, I plotted, then go downstairs to see if there is something from Holly. In a week I'd be flying to London with two fellow teachers. In two weeks I'd be in Paris, seeing Holly.

I went into the bathroom to empty the contents of the hamper into a cart, to take downstairs to the washing machine. Except for this minor chore I was ready this minute to step aboard the 747 that was scheduled to fly us to

1

London. My passport was in readiness, my wardrobe hung for last-minute packing. These final days before take-off would drag on forever, I guessed restlessly.

With the laundry deposited in the washing machine and churning its way to cleanliness, I took the elevator up to the lobby floor, walked down the corridor to the bank of mailboxes. Freddie was exchanging good-humored insults with a tenant awaiting his mail.

"Hiya, Janice," Freddie greeted me with a knowing grin. "You're gonna be happy. Got a letter from Rome."

"Great!" I charged down the line of open mailboxes, spewing forth vari-colored envelopes, to my own box.

I pulled out the usual assortment of bills, magazines, and ads. Within this conglomerate nestled an airmail envelope with Holly's return address. This morning I didn't dally for conversation as was my vacation-period habit.

The elevator door slid open just as I arrived in front of it. I hurried inside, pushed the button for my floor, and manipulated the mail so that I could slit the envelope containing Holly's letter. While the elevator moved upwards, I skimmed the opening of the letter.

"Darling, don't be uptight at what I have to tell you. At eleven this morning, Rome time, I was married! I've only known Jacques three weeks, but this is it, Janice. The Real Thing. Cancel that tour and fly out to stay with us at Jacque's villa. You fly to Paris, shuttle to Marseille, and pick up a rented car there to drive to the villa."

My heart pounding, I left the elevator, hurried down the corridor to my apartment. My hands were unsteady as I tried to cope with the double locks. My mind was trying to assimilate the knowledge that Holly was married—to someone she'd known only three weeks.

Holly, who is small, blonde, curvaceous, but with a mind like a Wall Street wizard, has fussed over me—five feet five and a hundred ten after a thick malt—ever since our parents crashed into Jamaica Bay four years ago. We were shockingly alone in the world—though according to Holly, I'd just acquired a brother-in-law.

Inside my apartment I reread the four pages of Holly's

large scrawl. They would be at the Villa Fontaine, forty-eight kilometers east of Marseille, on Friday. Tomorrow, my mind tabulated. Simultaneously, I tried to visualize the Villa Fontaine.

I was to book the earliest possible flight. Jacques would call the car-rental agency in Marseille where he maintained an account and arranged for a car to be available for me. Holly gave me specific instructions for reaching the villa.

"You should be able to get a seat quickly," Holly wrote. "The 747s never travel to capacity even in high season. I'm dying for you to meet Jacques. You'll adore him."

In less than an hour I had canceled out my planned tour, broken the news to my two scheduled traveling companions that they'd be seeing London and Paris *à deux* rather than *à trois*, and had acquired a seat an a 747 leaving JFK Monday evening. I'd breakfast at Orly Airport, catch a shuttle plane to Marseille and be at the Villa Fontaine in time for lunch.

Monday I handled all the last-minute details, like buying traveler's checks, moving my truly glorious coleus plants to a neighbors apartment for vacation care, and arranging for the super to hold my mail until my return. I suspected Holly might try to persuade me to stay as long as I could. She'd said firmly that Jacques and she intended to show me much of France.

Coming back from the bank, I collected my mail. There was an airmail card from Holly, dated Thursday.

"We're driving to the villa in this groovy red Ferrari," Holly wrote. "My wedding present. Wild, baby? We're stopping off somewhere tonight. We'll be at the villa tomorrow. See you soon."

Upstairs I dug out my Michelin to find the town from which Holly had sent the postcard. It was about fifty miles from the villa. Holly was in residence there now with her new husband. Tomorrow I'd be having luncheon with them. I felt like a jet-age Cinderella.

Far earlier than necessary I arrived at JFK, weighed in

my luggage, and went into the restaurant for a snack. I wasn't hungry. I was too keyed up about meeting Holly's husband to be interested in food, but it was something to do.

It was absurd to feel so strange in this situation, I chided myself. Holly was twenty-six and beautiful. What was more natural than for her to be married? But the three-week courtship made me faintly uneasy—plus the realization that Holly was now based in a villa forty-eight kilometers east of Marseille while I taught in a school in the South Bronx.

I was relieved when it was time to go to the boarding gate, to climb inside the giant 747 after the routine search necessitated by the recent wave of hijacking, and to settle myself in my economy seat.

It seemed that we were scarcely airborne before the stewardesses went into their tray-slinging routine. I toyed with my dinner, drank my coffee, declined the evening movie.

On either side of me passengers were settling down to snooze when the trays had been removed. My mind was too alert for sleep. A stewardess passed out light blankets. I accepted one, certain I wouldn't sleep one minute of the seven-hour flight.

In twenty minutes, overtired from the excitement of these past few days, I dozed off and slept most of the way over the Atlantic, until the breakfast trays were arriving. Breakfast time in Paris, perhaps, my mind telegraphed. Back in New York it was still the middle of the night. I settled for coffee.

I gazed excitedly from the window as we approached Orly. My first sight of France! Fleetingly I wished I could remain for a quick look at Paris. But that was ridiculous. Later Holly and Jacques would show me Paris.

Off the plane I waited in the crush to collect my valises, impatient now because I realized how close I was to Holly. A cacophony of French, German, Italian, English came at me from every side, a joyousness in the air.

Through customs with astonishing speed, I checked on

the shuttle flight to Marseille. A flight was scheduled to leave in twenty minutes. In an hour and a quarter I would be in Marseille.

The Air France flight connection between Paris and Marseille brought me into the airport at Marignane, northwest of the city itself. The day was grey, dismal, as it had been in Paris. I went immediately to the counter of the car-rental agency Holly had mentioned.

"I am sorry, Mademoiselle," the clerk behind the desk reported politely, "but there is no reservation in your name."

"Are you sure?" I stared in astonishment, "Please check again."

I waited, uneasy, while the girl behind the counter philosophically rechecked.

"No, Mademoiselle," she confirmed. "No reservation."

There must be a clerical error somehow, I decided. In the high season that wasn't surprising. But when I asked about acquiring a car without a reservation, the girl shook her head.

"We have not one car available. I am sorry."

Perhaps I ought to phone Holly. Jacques and she could probably drive out in an hour. But no, I stubbornly rejected this. Somehow, I must find a car rental and drive up to the villa on my own.

"Is there another rental agency here?" My eyes scanned the area.

"They are not likely to have a car without a reservation." The girl was sympathetic, thoughtful. "Wait," she exclaimed. I will call Marseille. Perhaps we can find a car for you."

In a few minutes the girl was back, smiling broadly. "In Marseille they will have a car for you. I will write out the address for you." She was already neatly printing this on a sheet of paper. "The taxi driver will take you there."

The sixteen-mile taxi ride into Marseille should have been a joy. The depressing drizzle that had commenced as I climbed into the taxi had given way in less than five minutes to brilliantly sunny skies. Yet I saw little of the countryside. I was impatient to see Holly, to meet her husband.

When I pick up the car in Marseille, I must ask for detailed directions to the villa, I thought, trying not to feel uneasy at the prospect of driving over foreign roads with strange highway codes.

In Marseille I took notice of the city as my taxi elbowed its way through the frantic maze of traffic, marveling at the way Marseille bubbled over with activity. The people—walking, sitting at sidewalk cafes, riding buses and cars—exuded a zest for living that was contagious. This, I recalled from a college course, was the city of tomorrow, with little truck for the past and tradition. Here Le Corbusier had designed a modern complex of apartments said to personify the dynamic quality of the city.

"Marseille, she is the second largest city in France," my taxi driver explained with pride. Reconciled to our slow crawl down the Canebière.

"It's a fascinating city," Now I stared avidly at the fabulous shops, the cafés that lined the avenue. Yet I felt an incipient alarm as I contemplated driving up the same wide traffic-congested avenue to the Rue St. Ferreol, via which I would leave Marseille behind.

Before the car rental agency I paid off my cab driver, and hurried inside to transact business.

"For how long, Mademoiselle?" the clerk asked while he pulled forth the necessary papers to be filled out.

"A week," I said unthinkingly. "I don't actually know," I corrected. I wasn't likely to need the car any longer than it took me to drive to the villa, but then the car must be returned to Marseille.

"It does not matter, Mademoiselle," the clerk soothed. "We will say for one week." He smiled encouragingly. "You may return it earlier and be charged accordingly."

With all the papers signed, my identification established, I asked for more detailed directions than Holly had supplied, inquired about local driving regulations. I knew my New York State license was sufficient.

"Is simple, Mademoiselle," the clerk assured me with

overt admiration. Apparently he flipped for skinny Americans with blue eyes, long honey-colored hair, and turned-up noses. "Just remember to keep to the right and overtake on the left. No speed limits," he said with pride, "except on weekends."

"Thank you." I smiled warmly. I had no intention of breaking speed records.

Cutting out of Marseille in the bright red compact assigned to me was less painful than I'd anticipated. I followed carefully the directions the clerk at the Marseille agency had plotted for me, grateful for the shortcuts which took me away from the highly traveled inland roads.

I sped along the Côte d'Azur, dazzled by the brilliance of the scenery, remembering that this had been the mecca for so many top-drawer artists —Matisse, Cezanne, Dufy, Van Gogh. Yet none, I thought romantically, could improve upon nature.

The limestone-chalk coast was fascinating. Across my mind teletyped a chunk of a travel book I'd skimmed a few days earlier. These deep bays along the coast were known as "calanques"—or drowned valleys. They reminded me of the fanciful stories my father used to weave about the ancient continent that is said to have once filled the Mediterranean.

Driving along the coast, I gazed to the north, awed by the wild mountain peaks in the distance, even now snow-capped, glittering in the Mediterranean sunlight. I watched for the fishing village—near a bay—which was my direction-finder. Once in the village I must stop to ask local directions. It would be easy to lose my way at this point.

More quickly than I anticipated, I saw the signs that indicated I was approaching the village. I drove into the business area, delighted with what met my eyes. How picturesque, with this earlier-century aura!

I parked, left the car to enter what appeared to be a general store.

"Could you give me directions to the Villa Fontaine, please?" I was pleased that I spoke fluent French.

The face of the woman behind the counter tightened with distaste as she stared at me, saying nothing.

"The Villa Fontaine," I tried again.

Deliberately she turned away from me and began to straighten a shelf of merchandise.

"Four kilometers along the road there," a man said, approaching me from across the store. "Turn left at the small white church. You cannot miss it. There is only one Villa Fontaine." His smile was sardonic.

"Thank you," I stammered, and spun about, anxious to be out of the store. The woman guessed I was an American, I rationalized. Some of the French were hostile towards Americans, particularly tourists. I could live with that, I decided philosophically.

I drove slowly, watching for the church. Four kilometers, the man had said. A kilometer was about five-eighths of a mile. I should be almost there.

Then I spied the church. Turn left, my mind instructed. I swung onto a narrow side road—modest houses, tin-roofed, surrounded by an abundance of flowers in rich bloom; then a stretch of openness. I leaned forward intently, sensing the Villa Fontaine would be just ahead.

A striking baroque structure rose on the side of a lushly green slope. Two wings jutted off from what appeared to be the main section of the villa, connected with this central portion via a network of terraces and balustrades. The late-morning sunlight created a golden silhouette of peaked roofs, dormers, chimneys. That had to be the Villa Fontaine.

Before the villa itself, elaborately terraced gardens spread forth, dotted with fountains and cascades. A cypress-lined road led through the gardens down to the stone wall that made a pretext of cutting off the villa from the public road. The stone wall was interrupted, just ahead, by enormous iron gates that swung slightly ajar, as though expecting an imminent arrival. An over-sized coat of arms with "Villa Fontaine" emblazoned in gilt was attached to a section of the wall. Anticipation warmed me. In a few minutes I'd be seeing Holly, after all these months, and meeting Jacques.

I braked, emerged from the car, shoved the gates wide enough apart for entry. Behind the wheel, I drove inside. The gardens were a fiesta of summer blossoms. A heady blend of scents drifted to me in the sea-washed air. Fleetingly I tried to identify the fragrances as I drove up to the villa. Mimosa and bougainvillea, I decided. And roses. I was in the south of France, a near-tropical climate. I smiled, remembering the expensive bottle of perfume which Holly had sent me from Rome, and which was tucked away now in the depths of my valise.

I pulled up at the entrance, and sat there intrigued by the splendor of the villa. Then my attention was diverted to a man on his haunches before a rosebush bursting with blooms. He handled the bush with a tenderness that was poignant.

He must have felt the weight of my gaze. He turned about awkwardly, stared at me, stood up hurriedly, and with a look of alarm headed away from the rosebushes.

Not a man, after all, I judged; probably no more than seventeen, astonishingly handsome. Yet, I'd been instantly aware of something odd about him. His eyes were frightened, uncertain. He was retarded. Compassion brushed me. I'd frightened him in his small, private world of the flowers.

I opened the car door, crossed to the stairs, walked up to the terrace that flanked the entrance. A rustling sound close by snapped me to attention. My friend with such affection for the roses was furtively watching me from behind a trellis. I smiled reassuringly. He ducked in fresh alarm.

I touched the doorbell, which seemed so incongruous set here in the entrance to this baroque masterpiece, and waited, a smile of anticipation lighting my face.

The door opened. A houseman inquired politely, "You are expected, Mademoiselle?"

"My sister expects me," I explained effervescently.

"Mme. Manet." He appeared startled. "Mme. Jacques Manet," I amplified. Perhaps Jacques's mother lived here.

"One moment, Mademoiselle." He ushered me into a vast, marble-floored, high-ceillinged foyer, graced by a wide, curving staircase. The staircase wall was hung with an impressive array of what instinct told me were genuine old masters.

I waited for Holly to come rushing down that magnificent staircase with that warm, faintly breathless manner of hers. Affection made this a special moment.

Instead of Holly, a tall, slender, attractive woman with near-black, elegantly coiffed hair and striking brown eyes strode lithely down towards me. The starkly simple, ultra-smart dress she wore must have cost as much as I earned in a month.

"I am Stephanie Manet," she introduced herself with faint reserve in London-schooled English. "You wish to see me?"

"I asked for my sister," I explained with a smile. Hadn't the houseman understood me? "Holly. Holly Manet."

Why was she staring at me this way? Almost with suspicion!

"Mademoiselle, there is no Holly Manet living here at the Villa Fontaine," she said with a touch of irritation. "I am afraid you have been given an incorrect address."

"Jacques's wife," I said quickly. My heart thumping. "My sister Holly." I sounded absurdly repetitious.

"I am afraid there is some mistake, Mademoiselle." She was politely sympathetic now. "My son Jacques is not married. My stepson," she amended with a faint smile, because I appeared startled by this relationship. Stephanie Manet was somewhere in her late thirties, I guessed. "Though after twelve years he seems like my own."

"I received a letter from Holly while she was in Rome. It was dated a week ago." I was struggling to hold onto my cool. "She told me that Jacques and she had been married that morning. They were driving back to the villa." In a red Ferrari that was her wedding present.

"They were scheduled to arrive here on Friday." I faltered, reading the disbelief in her eyes. "She told me to fly over to meet her here at the villa."

"What a cruel trick! Some young man has tried to pass himself off as Jacques. These things happen." Mme. Manet gestured expressively. "Jacques has a certain reputation. He is young, handsome, wealthy. Your sister is probably beautiful—this man wished to impress her."

"Holly is very bright. Very sophisticated." My voice was uneven, despite my efforts to sound unruffled. "I'd like to talk with your son, please."

"Jacques is not at the villa." Her dark eyes continued sympathetic, despite my note of skepticism. Perhaps because she sensed my alarm. "We expect him within the next day or two. Though, of course, he often doesn't show when expected."

"Would I be able to contact him by phone today?" Holly must be with Jacques, and they were keeping the marriage as a surprise.

"I don't actually know where Jacques is—" Mme. Manet frowned in concentration. "Perhaps his is at the Paris office. Let us call and find out."

She gestured for me to accompany her down the wide marble corridor with its impressive wall hangings, with exquisite antiques lining both walls, to the huge, beamed, shelf-lined library. How generous of her, I thought, to bother calling all the way to Paris for a stranger.

"Please sit down, Mademoiselle."

I sat in one of the black leather-upholstered chairs in this charmingly informal room, so unexpected here at the villa, while Stephanie Manet seated herself behind the expansive modern desk to phone. She spoke in brisk French to the long-distance operator, making the call person-to-person.

She drummed on the desk with one ringed finger, impatient with the delay in putting through the call. I sat tensely in my chair, feeling increasingly gauche in this situation. Yet I must pin down Holly's whereabouts. I knew

Holly was married to Jacques. Wherever Jacques was, there must be Holly.

Finally Stephanie Manet was speaking to someone in Jacques's office. Not to Jacques. She was asking questions, nodding slowly. My throat went dry when she put down the phone and turned to me.

"I am sorry. Jacques is not in Paris. He is incommunicado, even to me. He is working on a project with a research team." I didn't even know Jacques's profession, I realized.

I rose self-consciously to my feet.

"Thank you for your efforts. I'll find a room in the village and wait until he returns." I tried to sound casual. But today was already Tuesday, my mind pinpointed painfully. Holly said they were due this past Friday.

"The village people seldom rent out rooms. They are quite hostile to strangers. You would have to go into one of the nearby resort towns for accommodations. This time of year every inch of space must be rented out." She paused. "Mademoiselle, stay here at the villa until Jacques arrives," she invited with unexpected, ingratiating warmth.

"I couldn't impose that way," I stammered.

She smiled faintly. "I have a business arrangement in mind. Would you be interested?"

"Yes." My bankroll was hardly lavish enough to cope with French Riviera resort hotels. When I'd said I'd find a room in the village, I'd meant a modest *pension*.

"Later today I expect important business guests. My mother—who, by the way, is English—is . . ." She frowned, searching for a phrase. "How do you say in America? Slightly 'off' sometimes. Most of the time she is perfectly normal," Mme. Manet rushed to reassure me, "and then, quite suddenly, she will say the most absurd, the most embarrassing things. If you would agree to stay at the villa, to take your luncheons and dinners with her in her rooms, it would save me much discomfort. You will have most of your time free to swim, to sightsee. It will be a brief vacation." *With Holly off in limbo?* "Please, say you will stay," Stephanie Manet coaxed charmingly. "Jacques is so knowledgeable. When he arrives, I am confident he will be able to help you find your sister."

"Thank you." I managed a small smile. "I'd love to stay."

CHAPTER TWO

The impassive faced Edouard brought in my two valises—containing the wardrobe I'd so ebulliently assembled for my expected "two glorious weeks in London and Paris." While Edouard drove the red compact to the garage at the rear of the villa, Celeste—small, stocky, with inscrutable dark eyes and an air of covert disapproval—escorted me upstairs to my room.

Wrapped in an aura of unreality, I followed valise-toting Celeste up the lushly carpeted stairs. My mind tried to assimilate the knowledge that this impressive mansion was Holly's new home, though Stephanie Manet so thoroughly rejected my report that Jacques and Holly were married.

Mme. Manet was wrong, of course. Holly was not married to an impostor. She was married to Jacques Manet. And there was some logical explanation for their not being here.

Humor touched me briefly. If I were not so engrossed with the problems of teaching in a "troubled area" junior high, I probably would have recognized Jacques Manet's name, but the jet-set world was far removed from me.

Celeste paused before a door midway down the corridor, shifted a valise to allow her a free hand, thrust open the heavy, ornate oak door. With a small, polite smile I walked inside.

"Oh, how lovely!" I gazed about, intrigued by the charm of the huge room that sprawled invitingly before me.

The walls were beautifully covered with ivory damask, punctuated with groupings of small paintings in ebony frames. A marble-faced fireplace, laid in readiness for some unexpectedly chill evening, was flanked by a pair of tapestry-covered armchairs, between which sat an unexpectedly modern octagonal cocktail table with marble top. Tall, narrow windows brought a rich display of Mediterranean sunlight into the room. Between two windows sat a *bonheur-du-jour*, elaborately inlaid, with a shelf at the back. The chair accompanying it was upholstered, also, in tapestry.

The bed wore a sheer white canopy, was covered by a white quilted-satin spread and elegantly feminine dust ruffle. The base of the lamp on the night table was porcelain, exquisitely hand-painted. I was certain that the pair of rugs, utilized to indicate a sitting and a sleeping area, were priceless Aubussons.

"I will unpack for Mademoiselle." Celeste was carrying my valises to the walk-in closet. I suspected she harbored a strong, feminine interest in the contents of my unglamorous pair of valises. "You will have time for a nap before luncheon is served."

"I'd rather have a shower," I decided with candor. A hot shower would rest some of the tension from my shoulder blades.

"In here, Mademoiselle." Celeste reached to open the bathroom door.

The bathroom was half the size of my apartment back in New York. The tub, a rectangular chunk of marble, was sunk into the matching marble floor. The washbasin was lined in gold leaf, the faucets were antique gold. Deep green towels, hung in abundance, matched the green vein of the marble. No shower, I decided, discarding the sleekly designed stall shower for this movie-set tub.

I leaned over to run tepid water into the tub, listening to Celeste moving about in the bedroom, faintly guilty that I was about to soak in this gorgeous tub when Holly was missing. But again, I told myself that there must be some logical reason for Holly's absense.

Holly, with her penchant for exotic jobs, always kept me informed of her whereabouts. It was a compulsion with us to know where the other was—ever since our parents died.

I could go into the village, ask questions. A chill closed in about me as I considered this. Could there have been an accident with the car?

I started at the light knock on the door, barely audible over the rush of water into the tub. I reached to pull the door wide.

"Yes?" I was slightly self-conscious, not adapted to luxury living yet. Conscious, repetitiously, that Celeste harbored some covert disapproval of my presence at the villa. An extra guest creating additional work?

"Mademoiselle would like tea? Luncheon will not be served until two."

"That would be nice, Celeste." I brightened with anticipation. I'd had only a quick continental breakfast hours ago. "Thank you."

Celeste left. I lowered myself into the tepid, perfumed water, ordering myself to relax in this sybaritic luxury. Oh, Holly would adore the villa! When she arrived. *Why hadn't she arrived?*

I was too restless to linger long in the tub. I emerged from the water, wrapped myself in a green bathsheet, and, carefully drying my feet first, walked back into the bedroom. Celeste had laid out fresh underthings and my color-splashed jersey robe. My scuffs sat on the floor in readiness. I quickly abandoned the bathsheet, was just tying the robe sash about my waist when Celeste knocked lightly.

"Come in."

I might have been on some dreamlike vacation, except for Holly's absence. I sat down at a small table to have my tea, then slid out of the jersey robe into a mint-green linen sheath, returned to the bathroom to apply make-up and brush my hair. My reflections revealed none of my inner constraint.

Go on downstairs, I ordered myself. Enjoy my time here at the villa. Holly will arrive and everything will be all right again.

I deserted my room, walked down the hall, started down the staircase. Stephanie was at the door, talking with someone.

"Edouard has told you." Her voice was edged with annoyance. "M. Manet is away from the villa."

"But his public-relations office set this appointment for this afternoon," a male voice was insisting in American-tainted French. "I'm not trying to crash. Here are my credentials. I'm with *Modern Magazine*."

"I am sorry." Stephanie was icy now. "M. Manet is not available." Stephanie closed the door firmly, but not before I caught a glimpse of the caller. Tall, slim, informally dressed, with casual good looks. "Oh, these pushing magazine people," Stephanie said tiredly, aware of my approach now. "Always pursuing Jacques for interviews when he wants only to be left alone with his research." She shrugged her shoulders in incomprehension. "Come, let me introduce you to Maman. I have had a call from M. Carey. He will be here, along with M. and Mme. Whitney in time for dinner. Maman," she continued, "has a suite in the east wing, since her physician prefers that she not climb stairs. The housekeeper's rooms are directly behind, so that she is not alone."

We found Mme. Simone on the terrace off her sitting room. She was avidly reading a London newspaper. From the headlines I gathered this was one of the sensational tabloids. Stephanie frowned in annoyance while her mother hastily folded over the offending newspaper.

"Maman, this is Janice Carleton. She is staying with us for a few days. She'll be having her meals with you so you'll have company when those horribly dull business people return."

"Why don't we have luncheon here on the terrace?" Mme. Simone suggested with childlike eagerness. "It's such a lovely day." She leaned forward, a small, fair-haired woman who must have once been beautiful. But the blue eyes were fading, the fine English skin sagging with the passing years. "I don't like to eat in the dining room," she whispered. "I don't trust Celeste. I'm afraid she means to kill me."

"No, Maman." Stephanie was firm. I tried not to reveal my shock. Now I understood why Stephanie Manet wanted me at the villa. "Celeste will not hurt you."

Mme. Simone turned to me, seemingly mollified.

"You're so pretty, Janice. What a shame Jacques is not here," she said archly, shooting a conspiratorial glance at Stephanie.

"It would be lovely to have luncheon on the terrace." Stephanie Manet smiled apologetically at me. "But Celeste has already been instructed to serve indoors. Helene and Frederic are part of the regular staff, but the others are temporary. I had sent the others away for their summer vacation when I received word that these business guests were arriving." She turned to her mother cajolingly. "Maman, we should be going in."

"I'd like a cocktail," Mme. Simone said coquettishly, her eyes wary, expecting an argument.

"Maman, you know it isn't good for you." Stephanie tried not to appear exasperated.

"One cocktail will not injure my health," Mme. Simone said reproachfully. "I'd like a martini, please." A rebellious imperiousness in her voice. I could visualize Mme. Simone being difficult.

"Very well, Maman." Stephanie sighed, and turned to me. "Would you care for a martini, Janice?"

"Thank you, no." All at once I was impatient for luncheon to be over, to be in my rented compact and driving back to the village. Where I could begin to ask questions.

The three of us left the terrace and returned to the main wing of the villa. Stephanie led us to a small sitting room with bar facilities. While she prepared her mother a martini, and Celeste set the table in the dining room across the corridor, Mme. Simone talked about her girlhood in London.

"Everything is so different these days," she said wistfully. "There is so little dignity left in the world. I detest everything modern." She made a sweeping gesture with one heavily ringed hand.

"Not the Concorde-Prado," Stephanie jibed. "Friday Maman and I drove into Marseille." Instantly my mind pushed the "alert" button. "Every Friday we visit Maman's doctor in Marseille for her check-up. This past Friday we spent so much time shopping we were exhausted. We decided to stay overnight at the Concorde-Prado. It is Marseille's newest hotel. So very modern, so beautiful. And Maman, you adored it," Stephanie reminded triumphantly.

Stephanie and her mother were not at the villa Friday evening. Had someone tried to phone the villa about an accident, and nobody was here? But the servants must have been here, I reasoned. A message would have been left.

I listened politely to the feminine conversation, about clothes, shops, restaurants, but my mind was uneasy. *Where were Holly and Jacques?*

The American who had been at the door a little while ago expected Jacques to be here. Or was he lying, as Stephanie suspected?

Celeste appeared in the doorway to announce that luncheon was to be served. The three of us transferred ourselves to the sunlit, antique-furnished dining room. I ate with unexpected gusto, considering my frame of mind, the gourmet lobster bisque, the fluffy herb omelet, the chocolate mousse. I noticed Stephanie refrained from touching the mousse, and I guessed she was a calorie counter.

When Celeste arrived with coffee, I stole a surreptitious glance at my watch. Dinner would be served at eight. I must be back shortly before then.

After luncheon I went upstairs to my room to collect my purse. I felt a strained sense of urgency, yet subconsciously my mind dealt with small details: take along a sweater. Driving near the sea was apt to be cool once the sun began to descend.

Purse in hand, a grey cashmere cardigan across one

arm, I crossed to the window. Stephanie had explained that the stretch of beach across the road was private property, belonging to the villa. When the need hit me, I could lie on the white sand and enjoy the splendor of the Mediterranean in imperial privacy. *How* could I lie on the beach till Holly's whereabouts were pinpointed?

Suddenly I spied a figure strolling along the segment of beach in my sightline: a tall man in slacks and a sports shirt—the American who had been at the villa before luncheon. Why was he still on the villa property when Stephanie had so sharply dismissed him? Did he expect Jacques to show up this afternoon?

Go down to the beach. Talk to him. My heart pounding, I hurried to the closet, kicked off my shoes, replaced them with sandals that would be more comfortable for walking along the beach. I couldn't let him leave without talking with him!

Was he still there? I moved quickly to the window again, searched the ribbon of beach across the road. He was standing at the edge of the water, gazing off into the distance.

I hurried from my room, down the corridor, down the stairs. In the foyer I almost collided with a massive woman in a frill-free black uniform. At least six feet tall, with the bone structure of a college halfback. Deep-set eyes so forbidding that I recoiled.

"*Bonjour*, Mademoiselle." She nodded stiffly, walked away from me in her flat-heeled, sensible shoes, up the wide staircase. But the glint of naked distaste I'd seen in her eyes for an instant was unnerving.

"Do not be intimidated by Helene." Mme. Simone's voice, in a whisper inaudible to Helene, snapped me about to face her. She stood almost at my shoulders, a batch of magazines in her heavily veined hands. "Helene is always upset when strangers come into the villa. Because of Frederic."

"Who is Frederic?" I asked politely. But before she could reply, I guessed. The retarded teenager who worked in the gardens.

"Frederic is Helene's son." The pale eyes were aglow with relish at the chance to tell this story. "It is very sad. Frederic is not quite bright. He has the mind of a small boy. Stephanie allows Frederic to live here and work about the gardens to please Helene."

"I think I saw him before." How could I break away? I had to, before the American left the beach.

"Helene worked in a mental institution north of Paris as a girl." Mme. Simone glanced nervously up the stairs, but Helene was out of sight. "She was raped by an inmate. Frederic is the child that resulted. He's Helene's whole life. That big, stupid oaf. She dreams of taking him to America someday, where a brilliant surgeon will operate on him. We can't make her understand that nothing can be done." Mme. Simone shook her head in a lack of comprehension, while compassion chilled me. How easy it was to misjudge people, I reprimanded myself. Not knowing, I'd disliked Helene on sight—not knowing the tragedy with which she lived.

"I'm going for a walk along the beach." I grabbed at the opportunity to break free. "The Mediterranean is such a glorious sight."

I hurried down the long driveway, crossed the lightly traveled public road to the stretch of private beach. A pair of sailboats in the distance were incredibly graceful in the slight summer breeze.

At first I thought he had left, and disappointment billowed in me. Then I spied him, sprawled on the sand a hundred feet to my left, gazing fixedly at the horizon, mesmerized by the grandeur of the sea.

"Hi." Faintly breathless from exertion, I moved towards him.

He spun about in surprise. For a moment there was a hint of wariness in his brown eyes.

"Hi." Assessing me now. Speculating.

"I saw you up at the villa," I explained. He was far better-looking than I'd suspected from the brief sight of him through the opened door. I sensed a warmth in him, a lively interest, that immediately found a response in me. "I'm Janice Carleton, from New York."

"Neil Grant, from New York," he drawled with satisfaction. "Say this is great!" Still, I was aware of a lingering wariness. "Mme. Manet send you over to see why I was hanging around on her private beach?"

"No," I denied quickly. "I saw you from my bedroom windows. I knew you were an American." I hesitated. Was I making a mistake in telling him about Holly's absence? "I heard you talking about Jacques, about an appointment with him today," I plunged ahead recklessly. But don't mention Holly's marriage. It'll be sprawled all over the next edition of *Modern Magazine*. Let Holly tell him, not me. "I expected him here, too." I was trying to sound ingenuous. "My sister Holly wrote that she was driving to the villa with him on Friday. From Rome." Neil was watching me seriously. "Holly's an actress—she was in Rome, playing a small part in a film. I had a postcard from her—" Don't show him the card. It mentions the wedding. I sought in my mind for the name of the town nearby, mentioned it. "They were there on Thursday. I can't imagine why they didn't arrive at the villa the next evening." All at once I was trembling because of the alertness I felt in Neil Grant, the alarm I saw in his eyes for a moment before they went opaque.

"I had a definite appoint to interview him," Neil said carefully. "You expected your sister here last Friday. What did Mme. Manet say about that?"

I turned faintly pink.

"Stephanie Manet is sure that Holly's—" I hesitated, searching for a word. "That Holly's friend was somebody using Jacques's name." I paused, on the verge of confiding about the marriage. No, not yet. "But Holly's awfully bright. I can't believe she would be fooled that way."

"You came here to meet her?" Neil was trying to fit together the pieces I'd tossed at him.

"I flew out of JFK last night." I inspected him seriously. "Jacques and Holly were driving from Rome in a red Ferrari."

"There's probably some logical explanation for their delay," Neil said gently.

"I know. But all these days late? Still, you expected them here—and so did I. And they're not." I hesitated. "Do you suppose they could have had a smash-up with the car?"

"If there had been an accident, there would have been word at the villa. Jacques surely carried identification."

"I keep telling myself that, Still, I think I should check out the hospitals. And the local police station," I added with a tightness in my throat. But Stephanie Manet didn't believe Jacques was missing. The police would check with her. They'd dismiss me as a crackpot.

"Let me help you, Janice," Neil said gently. "I flew over specifically for this interview. It was set up by Jacques's public-relations firm to focus interest on a new fabric he's developed. This interview was to be a free, nationwide sales pitch in the American market. It was important to him."

"You suspect there's something wrong, too?" My eyes searched his, my own anxiety accelerating.

"We can't go wrong in checking," Neil hedged. "Do you have a photograph of Holly?"

"Two." I dug into my purse, brought out my wallet, flipped it open. "Here—"

Neil took the wallet, gazed intently at the two snapshots of Holly, both recent.

"Beautiful," he said quietly. "Like you."

I lowered my eyes. Why was I reacting like a nineteenth-century school girl to his compliment?

"Neil, how do we begin to search for them?" I asked earnestly, too unnerved at this point to think logically.

"We'll drive into the village. I have my car parked right down the road. For openers, we'll ask questions about a couple in a red Ferrari. And stop looking so desperate," he jibed gently. "Jacques and Holly would probably laugh their heads off if they knew we were so disturbed about their not showing on schedule."

Together Neil and I trudged over the white sand to the

public road. I listened absorbedly while he plotted our approach to tracking down Holly and Jacques. I knew it was absurd, but I felt such relief at having found Neil this way.

I couldn't know, then, the days and nights of anguish that lay ahead of me.

CHAPTER THREE

Neil settled me on the front seat of his rented black Renault, moved around the front to slide behind the wheel.

"My French is rugged," he warned humorously. "If I get stuck, can you bail me out?" But Neil Grant appeared capable of handling himself in any situation.

"I teach French in a junior high in the South Bronx," I confessed.

"You're putting me on," he jibed. "I went to junior high in the South Bronx. We never had a teacher like you."

"They're tolerant these days," I laughed. "They let me in."

"The best approach for us is to try the police stations," he decided, somber again. "We'll explain we're trying to track down your sister. You thought you were to meet her. She was with a friend in a red Ferrari." He wasn't mentioning Jacques. Did he believe—like Stephanie—that the man with Holly was someone masquerading as Jacques? "We'll ask if they have any reports of an accident involving a late-model red Ferrari."

"Could there have been an accident that hasn't been discovered?" The possibility was chilling.

"Not likely," Neil said firmly.

"Neil, when you contacted Jacques, was he in Rome?" I pursued.

"I don't know where he was at the time," Neil acknowledged ruefully. "The interview was arranged between my

27

editor and Jacques's public-relations firm. All I know is that I was to meet with him at the Villa Fontaine today."

We drove in silence the remainder of the four kilometers into the village. My mind grappling with a barrage of unanswerable questions. I realized from the mention of the Ferrari that Jacques was wealthy. The villa reiterated this. Only now did I realize that Jacques Manet was prominent in France.

"Neil, could Jacques have been kidnapped—and Holly with him?" I turned anxiously to him while he pulled to a stop before a low concrete building, its windows bordered with geranium-filled boxes. "Have you considered that possibility?" An unnerving thought.

"No," he conceded somberly. "But if they had been kidnapped, there would have been word at the villa. No," he said with a reassuring smile, "I'm sure they haven't been kidnapped."

"You talked about this new product Jacques has developed." My mind was chasing after a tangible lead. "Every once in a while the newspapers are full of some industrial spy plot. Maybe Jacques—and Holly—are being held by some industrial spy ring, because of this product. Neil, his office ought to try to track him down!"

"They don't believe anything's amiss," he reminded gently. His hand on the car door, he forced an encouraging smile. "Wait here," he said, "I'll go in to the *commissariat*."

"Let me go with you—" I moved forward, a hand on the door at my side.

"It'll be quicker this way," he insisted. "Wait in the car."

I sat back, my heart pounding. Neil was trying to protect me, in case there had been an accident. No, don't think that way. Don't let your imagination go dashing off on a roller-coaster.

I tried to concentrate on the trio of small fishing vessels off the shore. The brilliance of the sky, of the sea, was breathtaking. Don't think about Neil, inside the police station.

Why was he staying inside so long? It took only a moment to ask a question, receive an answer. What was he talking about in there? Despite my determination to keep my imagination in check, my mind was conjuring up painful images.

I sat up straight. Neil was emerging from the building. What had he learned? I tried to read a message in his expression.

"Did they know anything?" I called out anxiously.

"Nothing." Neil strode towards me, paused at my door. "I asked for the directions to the *commissariats* in the neighboring areas. We'll save time if we chart an itinerary." He hesitated. "Janice, would you be uptight if we stopped off for a snack? I haven't eaten since breakfast." His smile was wry. "I was supposed to have lunched with Jacques."

"Of course, have lunch." I was guilty that my initial reaction had been impatience with this delay. "I'll have coffee with you."

"I won't take long," he promised.

We drove down the road to the single block that was the business area, where I had stopped this morning to ask directions. Neil pulled up before a modest sidewalk café. A sprinkling of local citizens sat over glasses of cheap wine, enjoying the view, the piquant accent of the air.

We left the car, went to a table at the end. I was uncomfortably conscious of the cold glances beamed in our direction. We were tourists—to be tolerated, I assumed, for what money we would leave in the town.

Neil, feigning a lack of French, managed to communicate with the tall, heavy, perspiring waiter, who recommended the *bouillabaisse* with a sense of disdain, and went away appearing smug.

"The *bouillabaisse* will probably be loaded with fishheads," Neil guessed with a grin. His voice low. "But I wanted to get across the message that our French was nearly nonexistent. That way they'll talk openly. Probably unflatteringly," Neil warned. "We might pick up some tidbit that will be useful."

I was immediately attentive.

"Like what?"

"I don't know, actually. But sometimes something useful comes out of left field."

"Neil, last year at school a student of mine—a sweet, bright troubled girl—ran away from home. There were family problems—the mother refused to call the police. Maria had sent a postcard saying she was all right—but I was frantic. Her guidance counselor and I drove to Atlantic City—that was the postmark on the card. We found her, with the help of a snapshot in a fleabag of a hotel."

"You want to backtrack to the town where Holly mailed the postcard?"

"That's how we found Maria." I smiled in recall. "She'd been there for four days, scared to go back home. She'd been involved with a gang. I'd persuaded her to break away, and they were threatening her. Neil, the last contact I had with Holly was in this town fifty miles away. Maybe we can pick up her trail there."

"That's a good thought." He nodded slowly. "We'll try it. We'll inquire at the police precinct there, and all along the route they would take to the villa." His eyes rested on me with curiosity. "How do you happen to be staying at the villa?"

I explained the arrangement with Stephanie Manet, feeling unreal in this strange situation. But this was an era when everything was strange.

"Mme. Manet expects Jacques to arrive at the villa in a day or two. Then I'm supposed to be convinced that Holly and Jacques are not—" I stopped dead, color flooding my face.

Neil gazed quizzically at me.

"What about Holly and Jacques?"

I took a deep breath.

"This is not for publication," I cautioned. "I know you're a journalist, and Jacques is news—"

"Janice, right now I'm concerned only with finding Holly and Jacques."

My heart pounded as our eyes clung. It would be so easy to develop romantic ideas about Neil.

"Holly wrote me from Rome to tell me she had just been married. To Jacques Manet." Neil's eyebrows shot upward eloquently. "That was a week ago yesterday. I told Mme. Manet—I was sure she knew. She insists Holly married someone using Jacques's name. He's supposed to be incommunicado, on some research project. When I tried to convince her that Holly and Jacques were missing, she phoned the Paris office. They confirmed what she'd said."

"If he's incommunicado, why did his public-relations office arrange for me to come here to meet him?" Neil challenged. "If there was some last-minute switch, why didn't they notify my magazine?" He sighed in frustration. "Of course, it could have been some office goof-up." But neither of us believed this.

"Maybe Jacques told his Paris office he was tied up so Holly and he could have an uninterrupted honeymoon," I suggested romantically. But Holly expected to be at the villa this past Friday, my mind insisted on pointing out realistically.

"So Jacques Manet has left the eligible-bachelor list." Neil strove for a light note. "For the past three years he's been rumored to be involved with one European movie star or jet-setter after another."

"And along comes Holly, and she marries him." I tried for an air of matching levity.

Neil's eyes rested on me with an intensity that was disconcerting.

"I don't blame him for flipping, if she's anything like you."

"Holly's gorgeous." I'd never been drawn to anyone so quickly. "And she's very bright. Stephanie Manet ought to be delighted."

Neil's eyes glinted with amusement.

"It's kind of difficult to see Stephanie Manet as a mother-in-law. She's Jacques's stepmother, isn't she?"

"That's right."

"I'm not up on my jet-set gossip, but I understand she's a swinger."

The waiter waddled out with Neil's *bouillabaisse,* with my almond cresent and coffee, and waddled off again. Neil tasted the *bouillabaisse.*

"No fishheads," he said appreciatively. "It's great."

The sharp-faced Frenchwoman at the next table was dissecting the American tourist in malicious detail, while her bearded companion nodded in solemn agreement. Suddenly she stopped talking in midsentence. Neil, too, was engrossed with something out of my line of vision. I swung about curiously.

A gleaming, grey, chauffeur-driven Rolls was drawing to a stop before the café. The Frenchwoman was glaring at the two well-groomed men and the elegantly coiffed woman on the rear seat with a look of outrage.

"Charles, they are back!" she said furiously in French. "The Englishmen who came here before and carried on about buying the villa!"

Her companion appeared uneasy, gazed furtively at the three in the Rolls while the chauffeur approached a waiter to ask directions in shaky French. He was unsure about the road on which he was to make a left turn. The waiter pointed broadly, repeating directions with impatience. A left at the white church.

"Blanc," the waiter exhorted, and pointed to a white tablecloth for emphasis.

"Who is going to turn a small fishing village like this into a fancy resort and casino?" the woman's companion scoffed as the chauffeur returned to the Rolls. "A lot of talk."

"They have money," the woman hissed. "They can do what they will!"

"But M. Manet says he is going to build a factory in the village," he reminded defensively. "We will all have fine jobs. He has told everybody."

"A factory when these people come back again with their fat checkbooks?" The woman's voice was shrill. "M. Manet says one thing to make us feel good—and all the time he plans this resort. I tell you, Charles, there will be no village!"

"Janice, did you hear anything about the villa being sold?" Neil swung back to me.

"No." I frowned, trying to pin down exactly what I'd heard. "But Stephanie is expecting business guests—that was the reason for inviting me to stay. English, she said. They're due this afternoon."

"How awful, to transform this place into another resort," Neil said with distaste. "Do you blame them for being upset?"

"If the villa is to be sold, wouldn't Jacques have to be here? Surely he's involved."

"The villa may belong to Mme. Manet," Neil pointed out. "Or perhaps an attorney will show up to represent the family interests. Jacques wouldn't necessarily have to be present at the negotiations."

"I can't believe the Manets would allow that magnificent villa to be turned into a resort hotel." I shuddered as I visualized massive swimming opols, cabanas, new modern buildings with much glass, in shocking contrast to the baroque villa. And everywhere, my mind elaborated, swimsuited guests intent on diversion.

"For money even the Manets might bend that way," Neil warned with sardonic humor. "Obviously they have expensive tastes, and it must cost a fortune to keep up the villa, even with a wing closed off. The business is a multi-million-dollar corporation, but I understand profits haven't been up to scratch for the past three years. This is one reason Jacques was courting an American magazine with heavy circulation—for the free advertising for his new product."

The much-ogled grey Rolls was driving off in a spurt of dust. The woman at the next table rattled off a stream of invectives, not included in my French vocabulary. Neil grinned. I gathered his vocabulary, in some areas, was more extensive than mine.

Earlier than I'd anticipated, Neil and I left the café to climb into his Renault again. While we drove, Neil reminisced about his early adolescence in the South Bronx, then about the family's trek southward to the East Eighties as his father's earning power soared healthily.

"Mom still worries every time I climb aboard a jet," Neil said affectionately, and for a painful moment I remembered my parents' descent into Jamaica Bay. Holly and I had always been close, despite the five-year difference in age; but the tragedy lent a special urgency to our relationship. It was this feeling that brought me to the villa to meet Holly's husband. "Mom still worries because I don't have a 'steady job'," Neil mimicked tenderly. "It doesn't help to show her how income-tax day hurts me."

"Holly taught for six months. It wasn't her thing. She thrives on excitement. New places, new faces." A coldness clutched at me. How was she doing now? "She graduated Phi Beta Kappa, but to most people she comes on as a gorgeous ball of fluff. She's modeled, done some television—now she's having a fling at films." I hesitated. "She only knew Jacques three weeks when they were married."

"Whatever is delaying them, Janice," Neil soothed, "remember that Jacques is intelligent, resourceful, accustomed to thinking on his feet."

"I have this feeling that Jacques may be in some kind of trouble, and Holly's along for the ride. But when he doesn't show up at the villa this week—"

"We don't know that he won't," Neil interrupted gently.

"He won't." I insisted. Holly had said they'd be here last Friday. She'd move mountains not to upset me. *Jacques and she could not come to the villa. Why not?* "Maybe then Stephanie Manet will be sufficiently disturbed to start an investigation." With their money she could hire detectives.

"Let's try to come up with some leads." Neil forced a reassuring smile.

"They've been missing since Friday," I said bluntly.

"The thing that terrifies me is that nobody—except me—believes they're in trouble." Nobody, except for Stephanie and Neil, were aware of my suspicions, I acknowledged silently. But whom else could I tell? Jacques's office felt no concern. The American Embassy would insist I was a kook.

"I believe there's something wrong," Neil admitted. His eyes left the ribbon of road fleetingly to rest on me with compassion.

We drove along the fantastic roadway that flanked the sea, turned off after forty minutes onto a side road that led to the town where Holly had mailed the postcard. I sat in the Renault while Neil went into the *commissariat* to make his ghoulish inquiry, sat there with a sense of time pressing in around me, flattening me into cardboard.

Neil came out, shaking his head to reassure me he'd discovered nothing of tragic import.

"I've got our return trip scheduled," he said, sliding behind the wheel again. "If there's been an accident anywhere between here and the villa, involving a red Ferrari, we'll know about it."

We stopped regularly on our return trip. Each time I remained in the Renault, waiting with anguished uncertainty. No record of any accident involving a red Ferrari. I didn't know whether to be relieved or disappointed. If Holly were recovering from an accident in a hospital nearby, at least I'd know she was on the way to being all right, that she was safe. At this point I knew nothing.

Neil consulted his watch.

"It's late. I'd better drive you back to the villa. Will they wonder where you've been?"

"I don't know." I'd been too involved with finding Holly, I hadn't considered this. "Oh they'll probably think I've spent the day walking along the beach. I said I love to walk." I frowned in thought. "I guess I shouldn't volunteer that I've been with you all afternoon." My smile was faintly grim.

"I don't imagine Mme. Manet would appreciate that,

feeling the way she does about the American press. I'll
pick you up tomorrow morning near the villa gates.
Around ten. Or will you be sleeping late?" Unexpectedly
his eyes were humorous. "It shakes you up for the first
twenty-four hours or so, trying to adjust to the change in
time zones."

"I won't be sleeping late with Holly missing," I shot
back. But I felt a tiredness creeping over me, more from
anxiety than loss of sleep. "Neil, maybe it would be better
if I drove into the village, met you there?" He looked at
me with astonishment. "I arrived at the villa in a rented
car," I explained. "It's in the garage. They'll think I've
gone off on a sightseeing tour."

Neil appeared relieved at this suggestion. I gathered he
wanted to avoid any encounter with Stephanie Manet.

"Right. At the café," he confirmed. "I'll be there at ten
sharp."

CHAPTER FOUR

I walked briskly up the long, private driveway, my shoulders hunched slightly in protest against the new chill that brushed the sea-scented air, now that the sun was in descent. The villa stood out dramatically against the pinks and blues of pre-dusk.

Someone lingered, on haunches, at a flower bed far to the right, clipping away dead blossoms.

"Frederic!" Helene's voice, sharp and commanding, came from a window close by. "Frederic, it's getting cool. Come inside now."

I saw him rise awkwardly to his feet. The profile was astonishingly handsome, the body powerful and trim, yet as uncoordinated as a young child's.

"I am coming, Maman."

He didn't notice me. He moved without seeing in his eagerness to respond to his mother's summons, a poignance in his awkwardness as he hurried to the side entrance of the villa, as though just now aware that day was waning and fearful of the night.

I walked with an accelerated pace, conscious of my obligation as a temporary guests at the villa. Inside I went directly up to my room to wash up and change for dinner. I suspected that dinner at the villa, for Mme. Simone, was something of an occasion.

I was aware, again, of a growing exhaustion. Let dinner not be drawn out interminably. I yearned already to climb between the sheets and give myself up to sleep.

I was at the mirror, running a brush over my hair, pleased that I'd brought along a "little black dress" for such possible occasions as tonight, when I heard animated conversation—in English—out in the coridor.

"Oh, I was much too extravagant in Paris," a very British feminine voice was saying wryly. "Jim was quite annoyed with me,"

"Why shouldn't you be?" Stephanie challenged. "You have such exquisite taste, Celia." Stephanie siged. "I'd be extravagant, too, if we didn't have the horrible expense of keeping the villa in operation. This inflation is appalling. And it's so difficult to keep a decent domestic staff. Thank heaven for Helene."

"Perhaps the villa will soon be off your hands," Celia consoled. "Really, these places are so impractical as private houses in this generation."

The people in the grey Rolls, who had stopped at the café this afternoon—here to discuss buying the villa. The woman had been right.

Moments later someone knocked at my door. I crossed quickly to open it.

"Dinner will be served in ten minutes, Mademoiselle," Celeste announced. "In Mme. Simone's suite," she reminded with an undercurrent of maliciousness. I guessed she shared the villagers' dislike of American intruders.

"Thank you, Celeste," I smiled politely. "I'll be right down."

As I left my room I saw Stephanie start down the stairs with her guests, a woman with elegantly coiffed silver hair and a bone-thin figure in a high-fashion dinner dress— the woman who had sat this afternoon on the rear seat of the grey Rolls.

I couldn't see the two men. They were already halfway down the stairs. But I was certain they were the woman's companions of this afternoon. My job, I reminded myself, was to keep Mme. Simone out of speaking range of the high-powered English guests who came here with their "fat checkbooks."

I squinted at my watch again, in no rush to present myself ahead of schedule. From what I knew about Mme. Simone, this was certain to be a long evening spiked with much small talk, when I was growingly tense over being out of communication with Holly. By the time I arrived at Mme. Simone's rooms, I judged now, dinner would be ready to be served.

I walked down the wide, carpeted stairs, my mind focusing on Neil. Belatedly I realized I didn't know where he was staying. I should have, at least, asked for his phone number. But he would stay until Holly and Jacques showed. This interview was important to him.

A phone buzzed somewhere on the lower floor, was immediately answered. Approaching the foyer, I heard Helene summoning Stephanie from the library.

"M. Rochambeau is calling from Paris," Helene reported in her deep, masculine voice.

"At this hour?" Stephanie was upset. "Then he won't be here for dinner." She uttered a low sound of impatience. "Please tell Marie."

Helene moved towards the rear of the villa. Stephanie disappeared into the library, where I could hear the clank of ice in a cocktail shaker.

"Robert cannot be with us tonight," Stephanie was explaining as I passed the door en route to Mme. Simone's suite in the east wing. "Some case has detained him in Paris. Will you please excuse me while I talk with him?"

As I arrived at Mme. Simone's sitting room, I caught the pungent scent of burning birch logs. She sat in an ivory satin lounge chair at right angles to the crackling blaze, hardly necessary in this light chill brought in from the sea. Yet I relished the coziness of the fire.

How vulnerable Mme. Simone seemed, I thought compassionately, guilty because I'd stalled on coming down to her. She sat gazing with an interest I was sure was synthetic at one bejeweled hand, unconscious of being observed, talking softly to herself.

"Good evening," I called out with determined vivacity.

"Janice, how lovely you look." She leaned forward with eager welcome, her faded eyes brightening. I was glad I'd bothered to change for dinner. "And punctual. Most young people aren't these days. Though Jacques," she said with pleasure, "is exceedingly punctual." But he'd stood Neil up without a word. "That's because he's so earnest about his work," Mme. Simone pursued vaguely. "He's quite brilliant, you know. It's a shame his research keeps him away from the villa so much. He loves this house." She glanced up, nodded with a smile to Celeste—the sign to serve dinner. "It was so sweet of Stephanie to suggest we dine together this way." She had convinced herself that Stephanie was being solicitous. I was glad.

We sat down at a small, round, damask-covered table set close to the window where we could observe the sea in the distance. But Mme. Simone shivered slightly as she gazed out into the dusk, rose to cross to the windows, and pulled the drapes tight against the outdoors.

Dinner was elegantly French. Creamed filets of sole with oysters and shrimps, served with thin wedges of toast. Veal in red wine sauce. Asparagus with peas. Foie gras in gelatin. For dessert, when at last we arrived at that stage, a burnt almond pudding with coffee ice cream and macaroons. With it all a constant flow of trivial conversation from Mme. Simone.

She was flagrantly proud of Stephanie, her only child, and impressed with the importance of the Manet name.

"Stephanie's husband—Jacques's father—was a leader in the French Resistance. There is a room, at the turn in the corridor, where he kept all kinds of mementos of those years—the secret radios, the presses. I'll show you one day."

I ached to ask to see a photograph of Jacques. I'd looked about furtively, discovered none. I could phrase it casually, my mind plotted. Still, I couldn't bring myself to ask this.

"Paul died of a heart attack six years ago, when Stephanie and he had been married barely six years. It has been so hard on Stephanie, having to stay so much at the villa. She's accustomed to being free as a bird." Mme. Simone sighed. "But money is a problem these days, with everything so expensive. Last spring Stephanie was forced to close the east wing. Domestic help runs so dear—when you can find it."

The sale of the villa would bring an enormous amount of money. Stephanie could resume her jet-set activities. What about Jacques? How did he feel about the villa being sold? Mme. Simone said Jacques cared only about his work—yet she had said he loved the villa.

Was Stephanie, in some fashion, keeping Jacques away from the villa to make sure the sale went through? *Who had control of this?* Suddenly my heart was pounding as I considered the possibility that Stephanie was responsible for Jacques's and Holly's absence.

Stephanie had seemed genuinely shocked when I brought up the subject of Jacques and Holly's marriage. Did she know? Was this all a big sham, designed to make sure the villa was sold? No, I was being melodramatic, my mind insisted realistically. I was reaching for any explanation, no matter how illogical, in my anxiety to track down Holly. Stephanie Manet was not the kind of woman to resort to any kind of violence.

Where were Holly and Jacques? *This minute?* Alarm closed in about me. How could I sit here, enjoying this magnificent dinner, when I didn't know what was happening to Holly?

At the first hint of a yawn from Mme. Simone, I quickly suggested we call it a night: my first night at the Villa Fontaine. I felt oppressed at the prospect of sleeping in that exquisite room upstairs. Where was Holly sleeping?

Neil was right, I tried to convince myself. There must be some logical explanation for their absence. But with each passing hour I was more disturbed.

"A cup of tea before you go," Mme. Simone pressed with girlish enthusiasm. Her eyes warm with the pleasure of company. "I'll ring for the girl—" She frowned. "What's her name? Claudia?"

"Celeste." I'd have to stay for a cup of tea.

"Oh, yes. Claudia was a girl back in London." She smiled vaguely, mentally moving back into the days before she was Mme. Simone. Considerably less affluent days, I guessed.

Celeste arrived with a taut face that hinted at a concealed hostility, because she knew this job was temporary, lasting only until the regular staff returned from their vacations. Or was that hostility aimed particularly at me? The intruding American, who brought on extra work.

Mme. Simone and I pushed away another fifteen minutes over mint tea and more of Marie's excellent macaroons. Then I gently excused myself and headed for my room.

"Well, hello." One of the two Englishmen emerged into the corridor, smiled with approval. "I'm Phil Carey."

"Janice Carleton," I introduced myself self-consciously.

"Why is Stephanie keeping you secret?" he drawled. Blocking my path.

"Phil, what would you like to drink?" Stephanie demanded, her voice faintly sharp as she hovered in the doorway to the small sitting room. She smiled coolly at me. "Oh good night, Janice." I was being dismissed.

"Good night." I felt color stain my cheeks. I rebelled at being treated as though I were a member of her domestic staff.

Climbing the stairs, I could hear the lively conversation downstairs. Stephanie at her most charming, to compensate for the nonappearance of Robert Rochambeau, who, Mme. Simone had told me, was the Manet's attorney. She was questioning Phil Cary about his recent flight to South America. I gathered he had just returned yesterday.

I opened the door to my room, steeling myself for an entrance into unfamiliar darkness. I was childishly elated to discover that one of the servants had started a rousing blaze in the fireplace.

Nostalgically I remembered nights such as this in a cottage on Fire Island with Holly and a group of her entertainment-field friends. In Levis and sweaters we had trudged along the beach after dinner, returned to lounge before a roaring fire. The logs crackling as these crackled.

Now I was alone before a fireplace in a room that over-
looked the Mediterranean.

I moved about the room, switching on lamps. Seeking
comfort in brightness where normally I would have preferred only the glow from the logs. I crossed to a window,
pulled open the drapes, gazed out upon the night: only the
sea in view; the beach was deserted at this hour, the road
empty of cars. Below were the clusters of cypress, dark
and forbidding.

I left the drapes wide, somehow wishing to bring the
sea into the room. I closed the windows, though, against
the damp night chill, lingering briefly at the last window.
Why hadn't I asked Neil where he was staying? Neither of
us had thought of that. Now I felt a wistful urge to talk
with him, to hear the reassuring sound of his voice. Yet
even if I'd known, I wouldn't have risked calling him.
Stephanie Manet would be furious to know that I was on
friendly terms with Neil.

If Neil didn't show tomorrow, I wouldn't know where
to find him. Of course, he would show! We were meeting
at the café at ten. Why was I being so morbid?

Impatient with myself, I swung away from the tall, narrow window. Simultaneously, as I turned, I was conscious
of crashing glass close by, of a stinging pain at the side of
my head. I swayed, stunned by the impact of a blow, not
yet comprehending what was happening.

I lifted a hand to the side of my forehead. The fingers
encountering dampness. Blood! Something had broken the
skin. My eyes dropped to the floor. Glass from the shattered window lay in fragments at my feet. *Something else.*

I dropped shakily to my haunches, reached for the rock
that lay at my feet. A rock the size of a man's fist. A rock
that could kill.

Seconds ago I had stood there at the window, easily in-
dentifiable, I was sure, in the illumination from the lamps
about the room. The spill of summer moonlight . . .

Someone—down below in that cypress grove—had
thrown the rock with an intent to kill. *To kill me.*

CHAPTER FIVE

I stared at the rock in my hand. My head pounding. Blood on my fingertips, where they'd touched the wound. Not serious, my mind computed. It might have been fatal if I hadn't swung away from the window at just that moment.

Trembling, I switched off the lamps about the room, leaving it in the comforting shadows of the firelight. Now I moved to the window, avoiding the splash of broken glass at my feet. Nobody outside. Had I expected him to wait around? *Was he going to try again?*

Fix this cut—it isn't serious. I'm not going to need stitches. Wow, am I lucky! I could be lying dead now. Of no use to Holly. This *has* to be because I'm looking for her. Somebody heard Neil and me asking questions. They're afraid—because Holly is somewhere in this area. I know it now.

Trembling, I walked away from the window, painfully conscious of the shattered glass that tomorrow morning must be swept up. What would Stephanie think now? She must realize something was wrong. Not just Holly is in danger: Jacques, too.

In the bathroom I flipped on the lights, inspected my pale reflection. Blood welled from the cut at the side of my forehead, moving in an ominous trickle down to my cheek. My head pounded.

I reached for a wad of tissues, wet it, touched the wound. Clean it, my mind ordered. No glass to worry about. A clean cut from the rock.

For a moment I struggled against panic. Why didn't it stop bleeding? Pressure. Apply pressure. Standing there, the tissues hard against the cut, I fought down an impulse to try to phone Neil. What could he do? Whoever had thrown that rock was far away by now.

The blood stopped. I went out to the closet wall, reached into my weekender for a supply of bandages and drew out the bottle of aspirin at the same time. I'd never sleep tonight with this headache. For a few minutes I was occupied with the prosaic necessities.

All right. I have to go downstairs now, explain to Stephanie what happened. Will she call the police? They probably have no more than one policeman in the village—what can he do?

Instinct warned that Holly would not be helped by a village policeman. Private detectives. From Marseille perhaps. Let Stephanie call in private detectives. They could check out the marriage—wherever it took place. They know how to do these things. Then Stephanie would believe that Holly and Jacques were missing.

Except for the square bandage there at the side of my forehead, I looked normal, I decided after a searching inspection in the mirror. What will the others think—Stephanie's guests, the servants? I'd better not talk in front of Stephanie's guests. The attack on me might frighten Celia Whitney into leaving.

Go over and draw the drapes tight. They'll make the chill night air less penetrating. With a shiver of distaste I crossed to the shattered window to pull the drapes shut, moved to the other tall, narrow windows to repeat this. Only then did I switch on a lamp beside my bed.

I opened the door. Voices trailed up to me from the foyer. Stephanie's guests gathered there while they waited for a car to be brought around to the front.

"Stephanie, I do wish you'd come to the casino with us," Celia was saying persuasively. "You adore roulette."

"A woman's game," Jim Whitney derided. "You're all impressed with the glitter of gold and the colorful felt."

"Not tonight," Stephanie demurred. "Robert will call me after his meeting."

"Make sure he understands," Phil Carey said heavily.

"Our people are impatient with these delays. This is absolutely our final offer. Why is Robert so slow?"

"He's terribly busy right now." Stephanie was anxious. "But he's drawing up the contracts. He began to work on them last week, when you called."

"Robert and you can act alone on this contract?" Jim Whitney questioned quietly. "We don't need to wait for Jacques to sit down with us?"

"Jacques has been notified about the sale. He's just ignored my letter. I can't get through to him—he's tied up on another research problem. But it doesn't matter," Stephanie emphasized. "While Robert would prefer to have Jacques part of the negotiations, he's prepared to go ahead without Jacques. Robert will be available, with the contracts. You will have ample time to go over them. By Sunday night," she prophesied, "your syndicate will own Villa Fontaine."

"Stephanie, you won't change your mind and come with us?" Celia tried again as a car pulled up before the driveway. "I promise you, there won't be another word of this dull business talk the rest of the evening."

"Not tonight," Stephanie apologized. "I must stand by for Robert's call."

I waited until the door closed behind Stephanie's guest, then went down the stairs.

"Mme. Manet—" My voice was faintly breathless from efforts to sound casual. Stephanie swung about with a politely inquiring smile. But she was upset. "The craziest thing just happened. I was standing at the window, looking out at the sea—and a rock about as large as my fist—" I pantomimed graphically, "—came crashing through the window." Her eyes found the bandage at my forehead. She was pale with shock. "I'm afraid the floor is covered with glass."

"Are you all right?" Her voice was uneven.

"Just a scratch. I moved at the right moment."

"It was meant for me, Janice." Her eyes were terrified. "They hate me in the village because I plan to sell the villa. They can't bear progress. Somebody meant to kill me tonight because they've seen M. Carey and the Whitneys about the village. They know the sale is close at hand."

"No," I stammered. "I was standing in the light—the drapes were pushed open. They could see me clearly."

"From down in the garden?" Stephanie shook her head in rejection of this. "Whoever threw the rock aimed for me. We're the same height. At a distance we could be mistaken for each other. Janice, I'm so sorry—"

"There's no way of catching him now," I said somberly. "He's probably far away."

"No point in calling the local police." She smiled dryly. "He would have to stumble over a burglar before he caught one. But you can't sleep in that room tonight with the window broken. I'll call Helene to prepare another room. And she'll bring us coffee in the library. We can both use it." Stephanie took a step down the corridor. "Helene—"

Helene listened with impassive face to Stephanie's report on the rock-throwing. I churned with fury because I sensed she was amused. But why did Stephanie insist on believing the rock was meant for her? Couldn't she understand that somebody meant to freighten me away from the villa? Or to kill me? Because I was searching for Holly and Jacques . . .

Over coffee in the library Stephanie talked candidly about her eagerness to be free of the villa, to be able to travel at will.

"Here one must go into Marseille to shop for the smallest articles," she said with disdain. "More often I fly to Paris. Robert agrees with me it would be most practical to sell when we have such an attractive offer. But the villagers are furious. They don't understand that their own lives will be improved by the money that will come in with the resort opened up. There are so few opportunities in the village now. Only the fishing. They would benefit. That rock-throwing tonight—" Her face grew taut with anger. "That shows you how furious—and how stupid—they are."

A phone rang somewhere on the lower floor. Stephanie excused herself to pick up the extension in the library.

"Robert—" She smiled brilliantly, her voice laced with affection. "I hoped you would call. Will you hold one moment, please?" Stephanie covered the phone, turned to me. "Janice, you will want to change for the night. I'll send Helene up to call you when your room is prepared. It is not so lovely as the one you have, but it will do for one night, yes?" Her smile was ingratiating. "Tomorrow the window will be repaired—and I will phone Marseille about a night watchman." She sighed heavily. "More expenses to keep the villa running."

"Good night." I tried to be casual about this second abrupt dismissal. Yet it was natural that she wished for privacy in which to talk to the attorney. Mme. Simone had hinted earlier at a possible romance.

I went back into my room with a discomforting inner reluctance. Nothing else was going to happen tonight, I sternly reproached myself, and embarked on my bedtime preparations. *When* was it going to happen again? The insidious question nagged at me. I was sure there would be other attempts to frighten me away from France. Or to kill me.

In pajamas and robe I stood before the heat-wrapped logs in the fireplace. More for comfort than warmth, though a wet chill came into the room through the broken window. Outside a fog rolled in from the sea, closing eerily about the villa.

I started at the knock on the door.

"Come in."

The door opened. Helene's massive bulk moved into view.

"Your room is ready, Mademoiselle. Will you come, please?"

"Thank you."

I knew it was absurd to be intimidated by Helene. She lived with tragedy. This was her defense. With a small, tight smile I followed her down the corridor, walked into the room she indicated. Obviously, it had been long closed up. Helene had thrown open the windows to lessen the mustiness that assailed our nostrils. A fire was lit, the bed neatly turned down.

"Do you wish the windows closed, Mademoiselle?" An unexpected note of solicitude in Helene's voice. As though she were suddenly conscious of the earlier mishap. The smashed window.

"Thank you, I'll close them later." I smiled faintly. All right. Helene was offering a truce.

I stood before the fireplace, restless, too keyed up to sleep. The two cups of coffee I'd just consumed were not conducive to slumber, I jibed inwardly.

On impulse I crossed to the window. Feeling an odd protection in the blanket of fog that rolled in about the villa. Visibility was no more than a few feet. Despite the chill in the air I walked out onto the wrought-iron-railed balcony.

Stephanie's voice drifted up to me.

"What does it matter that Jacques isn't here, Robert? I've written to him that I wish to accept this new offer—he simply ignores me. If you vote with me, we don't need Jacques—the sale can go through. I tell you, they are becoming very impatient with these delays." She was silent for a moment, obviously listening to Robert. "Oh, Robert, it's absurd for Jacques to be concerned about changes in the village. We can't remain in the last century. Robert, with this stupid inflation, we can't afford to lose out in this sale. It's a fantastic offer—you know that. If Jacques wanted to stand in the way, why isn't he here?"

Stephanie wasn't concerned about Jacques showing up at the villa. *She didn't want him here.* All she needed to do was to persuade Robert Rochambeau to vote with her, and the sale would go through. I turned cold with alarm as I considered the situation. Jacques, here at the villa, could kill the sale.

"Oh, Robert, I've hired an American girl temporarily as a sort of part-time companion to Maman. To keep her occupied while the Whitneys and Phil Carey are here. You know she can say such embarrassing things. It isn't costing me anything—the girl is glad to have living accommodations while she's here."

My face hot, I moved back into the room, shut the window tight against Stephanie's voice. Insidiously, suspicions about Stephanie's part in Holly's and Jacques's disappearance crept into my mind.

For a long time I sat before the smoldering fire—knowing sleep would be hard to come by tonight, more convinced than ever that Holly and Jacques had met with foul play—and that Stephanie Manet was involved.

I came awake suddenly. With a sense of plummeting through space. Sunlight filtering through the shut drapes. What time was it. Had I overslept?

I struggled into a semi-sitting position, leaned over to focus on my watch, prone on the night table. A few minutes past nine. I was to meet Neil in the village at ten. Time enough.

I swiftly thrust aside the summer blanket, slid my feet into the scuffs at the side of the bed. A slight, dull pain in my head brought last night's near-catastrophe into glaring replay in my mind.

With distaste I realized I'd have to go back into that room to dress. Childishly, I wished I didn't have to go in there until the broken glass was swept away. Until that window was repaired.

Would Celeste automatically bring my breakfast into that other room? No, she would wait for me to ring. Would she know about last night? I turned this over in my mind. No. Helene would never gossip with the temporary staff. Let me dress quickly, get out of this house. I could have breakfast at the café with Neil.

With a sense of urgency I pulled on my robe, hurried from the bedroom into the corridor. No sign of activity upstairs. Obviously everyone slept late. Downstairs Helene was instructing Edouard to take down a pair of drapes which must be sent to the cleaners.

I hastened down the corridor to my original room. At

the door I geared myself for that splash of glass on the floor. Feeling faintly sick as I stared at the rock, still lying where I had placed it. No one had been in to clean up the debris yet.

I showered quickly—no luxurious tub today—and dressed. I hurried out of the room with a childish hope that I could leave the house without encountering anyone.

"Mademoiselle," Helene's voice—deep, reproachful— cornered me at the foot of the stairs. "You did not ring for breakfast."

"I plan to spend the day sightseeing," I stammered. Apparently Helene had decided I was no hazard to Frederic. She was anxious to be friends. "I'll stop on the way for breakfast." Last night Mme. Simone had confided that today she was going on one of her health fasts. She would remain in her suite resting all day, drinking only liquids. Therefore, I was off the hook until dinner.

"Madame would be most disturbed," Helene rejected this. "I will have Marie prepare a light breakfast. Celeste will serve you on the east terrace." She opened a door to a small sitting room. "The terrace is through there, Mademoiselle."

I couldn't refuse. I couldn't say, "I'm sorry—I have an appointment in the village." If Stephanie knew I was seeing Neil, she'd toss me out of the villa. Considering the state of my traveler's checks—and the cost of living in the village, if I could have found a room—I needed this arrangement. I didn't know how long it would be necessary to remain. I shivered, thinking of Holly—out there in limbo.

On the terrace, I seated myself at the heavy pine table that would accommodate a dozen people, glancing anxiously at my watch. I have a compulsion to be on time. Let this breakfast bit not drag out interminably.

The sun was high already. Last night's fog was a memory. I glanced restlessly about at the magnificent gardens that spoke of loving care. My eyes stopped their sweep to rest on Frederic, who stood beside an azalea bush, staring hard in my direction. I smiled tentatively. All at once, he was alarmed, moved awkwardly about with that splendid body of his, and disappeared. Poor Frederic. Poor Helene.

In a matter of minutes a sour-faced Celeste was shuffling out onto the terrace with a tray. A small white bone-china pot of coffee, a matching plate bearing an assortment of croissants and pastry. I ate with record speed, impatient to be behind the wheel of the rented compact and en route to the café where I was to meet Neil.

I left the terrace, took what appeared to be a shortcut to the garage. As I strode along the path I saw to my right—her back was to me—Helene with a washcloth in hand, washing Frederic's face with the tenderness she might have shown a much-loved five-year-old. I felt guilty at my hostility towards Stephanie—who had the compassion to allow Helene to keep her son here.

The garage was large, unexpectedly modern, with living quarters above. Helene and Frederic lived in the villa. The temporary staff utilized these quarters, I surmised.

"Come on, Phillips, you can do better than that," Edouard was jibing, and then swung about in heavy silence as he became aware of my presence. He was playing cards with the Whitneys' chauffeur.

"Good-morning," I said self-consciously, aware of their veiled hostility. "I just came to take out my car."

"You could have called, Mademoiselle," Edouard said coldly. "I would have brought your car to the door." He was annoyed that I had come to the garage. For an instant I felt gauche and defensive. I wasn't geared to this high-style living.

Edouard pushed back his chair, his face sullen, strode across to a wall plaque containing car keys. Silently he handed me my own. I murmured politely, climbed behind the wheel of the red compact. Discomforted by the awareness that the two men were watching me as I drove out of the garage and down the driveway to the road.

I arrived at the café exactly at ten. Breathlessly, I parked, left the car, walked to a corner table at the outdoor section. The one waiter on duty was the man who had been so arrogant to Neil and me yesterday. He stared hard at me, turned his back, and disappeared inside.

I was the only patron except for a pair of middle-aged Frenchmen taking their continental breakfast. I tried to interest myself in the picturesque village street—how colorful, the iron grillwork that adorned the low cement buildings, the flowers, particularly geraniums, in such dramatic abundance. A water trough about twenty feet to my right bore the date 1798.

What would happen here when the villa became a resort, catering to those with expensive tastes and matching pocketbooks? Would the town suddenly be overrun with fancy boutiques, elegant restaurants, and fancy cocktail lounges? Would traffic be charging through these streets where dogs casually sauntered now, confident that the occasional cars would avoid them? A lone rooster, I noted with amusement, was taking a solitary walk down the street.

Jacques had promised the villagers he would build a factory here. Fishing was not enough to earn a living these days. Now, they so quickly suspected, he was ready to sacrifice the village for the sake of a fabulously high price for the villa. Did they have so little faith in him?

The waiter emerged again. He walked to the pair of Frenchmen.

"The girl from the villa is here again," he said with contempt. "Flaunting herself before us! At least, she should know enough to keep out of our sight!"

I felt my face grow hot. He thought he was safe, speaking his native language. Now he wiped a table, continuing to ignore me, expecting me to become angry enough to leave.

I remembered Ralph, a troublesome student last year, who had ignored every instruction I gave him that harrowing first month of my teaching. I'd gritted my teeth, listened to the advice of veteran teachers, and fought to cope. This waiter was not driving me away from the café, no matter how much he hated those who lived at the Villa Fontaine.

I left my table, walked to him with a deceptively sweet smile.

"Monsieur, I am sure you are unaware that I've been waiting to be served for fifteen minutes," I said in French too fluent to be ignored. There, that shook him up! "Please bring me coffee and a croissant. I'm sitting right over there." I indicated my table, and without a backward glance, returned to it.

With surprising speed my coffee and croissant arrived. What was keeping Neil, I wondered now? Should I have kept silent about Holly's marriage? Neil wouldn't misuse that information. I couldn't believe that.

I needed Neil's moral support now, the way I'd needed the guidance counselor's at school when I was tracking down Marie.

Then I spied Neil. He waved at me as he emerged from the Renault. With a sigh of relief I waved back. He strode across the street to the café.

"I'm sorry to be late." He slid into a chair across from me. "The Renault conked out eight miles down the road. I went in to this place—my gas line was plugged. All I needed was an air hose job—it would take minutes. But I'm an American," he reminded wryly, "so he tried to hold me up for a major overhaul. Leave the car till tomorrow, he tells me, so I can run up a five-hundred franc tab. I took the car down the road, told the guy exactly what I wanted, and he did it." Neil snapped his fingers. "Just like that." He pantomimed to the waiter to bring him coffee. The same waiter who had pointedly ignored me until I'd given him schoolteacher treatment, responded with alacrity. Neil squinted at the square bandage on my forehead. "What happened to you?"

"It sounds crazy," I warned. "Somebody tried to frighten me away from the villa last night—"

"What's happened?" Neil wasn't laughing.

As calmly as I could manage, I reported last night's happenings.

"It could have been somebody out for Stephanie," Neil backed her up. "Feelings run high here against her because of the possible sale of the villa. Her husband was a kind of local hero in the French Resistance, which makes them doubly indignant."

"But Neil—" I began intensely.

The Manet plant in Paris is not in the healthy financial position it was three years ago—due in part to the fact that Jacques has instituted so many employee benefits. Stephanie has been feeling the pinch." He paused. "I've been doing some digging. I understand she's in hock at the gambling casinos. She must raise cash to get off the hook. They know she's determined to make the sale."

"But whoever threw that rock saw *me*. I had every lamp in the room lighted. Moonlight was spilling all over the place. The fog didn't roll in until an hour later. Anybody would have had to be blind to mistake me for Stephanie!"

"What was her reaction?" Neil asked somberly.

"She thought what you did," I admitted. "That the rock was meant for her." I lowered my voice. The woman at the next table was trying to eavesdrop. I couldn't take a chance on her not understanding English. "Stephanie is bringing in a night watchman from Marseille—she's that disturbed."

"But not for you," Neil guessed cynically. "Look, Janice, we don't know for sure whether the rock was meant for Stephanie or you. To be on the safe side, you ought to cut out of the villa right now. Get away from the village. They may suspect you of being involved in the sale, for all we know."

"No." My eyes flashed with refusal. "I can't run away."

"You're going to sit there and let somebody take another crack at you?"

"Whoever threw the rock last night isn't going to come charging around the villa with a watchman on the prowl," I pointed out with a confidence I didn't feel. "At least, now I knew to be careful." Of whom? Of what? Stephanie? Some psychotic villager?

The waiter came towards us with coffee. We lasped into temporary silence. He was respectful now, I thought, but the hostility had only gone underground. I belonged to the Villa Fontaine.

"Let me have those snapshots of Holly," Neil asked briskly. Instantly I drew out my wallet, removed the photos, my eyes questioning. "We're going to do what you did with that girl. Check the hotels in the town of the postmark. What time must you be back at the villa?"

"Not until seven-thirty."

Neil dug into his jacket pocket, pulled out a map of our vicinity. He spread it out on the table, inspecting it somberly.

"Here." He marked the town from which Holly had sent the postcard. Then he made a half-circle of the area within fifty miles, indicating what we must cover.

"Okay, finish up your coffee," he ordered briskly. "We'll cut out."

The town where Holly had mailed the postcard was a fair-sized town with three hotels. We spent forty-five minutes flashing Holly's photos, asking questions, and came up with nothing more than flattering remarks about her looks.

"If anybody had seen her," I conceded ruefully when we emerged from the last of the three hotels, "he would have remembered. Holly's spectacular."

"Okay, so we bombed out in this town," Neil said matter-of-factly because I was uptight. "We've got plenty more places to cover. But we might as well stop in somewhere for lunch. Everything's closing tight for the two-hour luncheon scene." He smiled faintly. "Except the restaurants."

We decided to drive to the next town, quite small but boasting a hotel. We found a restaurant on the main street, went inside. A friendly, rotund waitress came towards us with surprising grace considering her bulk, and handed us each a menu.

"Interesting," Neil commented humorously, surprised as I was at the modest prices.

When lunch arrived, we were even more impressed.

First a huge tureen of soup—from which we were to serve ourselves—and a platter generously piled with bread.

"Hmm, sensational," I murmured with respect, sipping the thick, savory soup. "I could make a meal out of this."

"Sometimes you hit a small town and the prices are right and the people great. I know a spot like this about thirty-eight kilometers out of Geneva. Aubonne," he said reminiscently. "On the side of the mountain in vineyard country. What beautiful people! But if you go into Geneva and the large towns—and you're American—watch out." He whistled eloquently.

We ate with no sense of rush, and heavily—pork chops, mouth-watering roast potatoes, and a salad followed the soup—because in these towns it was impossible to approach people during the long luncheon period. But all the while unease tugged at me. Why did I have this odd feeling that I was painfully close to Holly?

Was she somewhere in this town? Was she all right? Why were they holding Jacques and her this way? That vague, unidentifiable, frightening "they."

My appetite for luncheon fizzled away. Holly would never have told me she'd be at the villa—and then not show. *Not unless she was being held against her will.*

Holly and I have this mutual hang-up about always keeping in touch. When our parents crashed, I'd spent eleven anguished hours trying to catch up with Holly, who'd been off on a weekend with friends. That scarred us forever.

"Janice, you've left me," Neil called quietly. "Come back."

"I'm sorry." I forced a smile. "I keep thinking about Holly—"

"I talked to my magazine last night," Neil said gently. "They've okayed my hanging around here for a week." I started. Would it take us that long to track down Holly? I wouldn't consider *not* finding her. "I asked if they had a contact in Rome who might be able to do some research—"

"You told them about the wedding!" I stared in shock.

"No," Neil said quickly. "I figured if they had somebody in Rome, he could do some checking around—"

"To see if Holly and Jacques are actually married?" I cut in, color staining my cheeks. "I'm not concerned about that now. I want to find Holly." Neil wasn't sure about their being married. Childishly, I felt betrayed.

"Janice, the marriage is part of the whole picture," Neil said earnestly. "Someone on the scene in Rome could make some discreet inquiries in Rome and the surrounding area—"

"And once you knew for sure, your magazine could run an exclusive on Jacques Manet's marriage!" The pieces zapped together in my mind with jeering clarity. I pushed back my chair, leapt to my feet. "That's why you're so anxious to confirm the marriage. For a story for your magazine!"

Tears stinging my eyes—too uptight to rationalize—I stumbled away from the table, rushed for the door.

"Janice!" Neil's voice followed me.

"Monsieur!" the waitress protested, and there was the clatter of china as our coffee hit the floor.

"Janice!" Neil called. "Janice!"

CHAPTER SIX

I hurried out of the restaurant into the torpid heat of the July afternoon, fled as though pursued by a pack of bloodhounds, hearing the waitress's high-pitched reproach because Neil's sudden rise from his chair had upset her tray. His apologies provided me with time to escape.

I turned into a narrow street with sidewalks wide enough for one, spied a window-draped restaurant—it was also the local movie. My heart thumping, I darted inside, made my way to a corner table wrapped in shadows.

A waitress came over. I ordered a pastry and coffee. Grateful for the dim illumination, the heavy draperies at the window.

"Janice!" Neil's voice, somewhere on the wide, main street above. "Janice?" The natives must be thinking, "Ah, another crazy American."

I sat stiffly at the edge of my chair. Wow I'd been naïve!—romantically thinking Neil was anxious to help me. It was just part of his job. *He was using me.* And I'd flipped for him.

How do I get back to the car? There must be a bus service somewhere around. I'll ask the waitress. In a pinch I can find a taxi.

Suddenly I was conscious of curious glances from the other diners. They knew I was a tourist. They always know. I tried to concentrate on my surroundings, to ignore my thumping heart. The people in here worked in the area, I guessed. At night those heavy drapes across the room were probably drawn aside and this became the movie house. How quaint!

61

Where's Neil? He's probably searching all over for me. He won't think of coming in here. He was lying, wasn't he, when he said he hadn't told the magazine that Jacques and Holly were married? That's all that has concerned him from the beginning—picking up a hot story.

Suddenly, disconcertingly, doubts assailed me. I didn't want to believe Neil had no personal interest in me. All right, break this down realistically. Neil's job is important to him—he wouldn't have been hanging around the beach that day if he hadn't been trying to figure out how to grab that interview with Jacques. But would Jacques's *marriage* be a story for the magazine?

I sat back, pondering this angle. Actually, it was Jacques's discovery of an important new fabric that was going to be the substance of the article. I'd jumped to conclusions, my mind denounced. Acting—again—on impulse.

The waitress returned with my pastry and coffee. I tried to pretend interest. The customers were thinning out, going back to their jobs. Where was Neil? I pushed down an instinct to go and search for the Renault. No. No, I can't! Not after I've made such an idiot of myself.

Neil has Holly's photos. The only ones I brought along. That's a solid excuse for calling him. What luck he gave me his phone number this morning!

I'll apologize—but he's probably furious with me by now. Maybe he's cutting out on the whole scene. Oh, I've messed up on this—when Holly needs me so badly.

"More coffee?" the waitress inquired, her eyes mildly curious.

"No, thank you." How did I get back to the village? "Is there a bus station here in town?" I asked self-consciously.

She explained there was no station. Late in the afternoon a bus would stop two blocks down, going in my direction.

What would I do till late afternoon?

"Is there a taxi?"

"That would be very expensive," she said, frowning in

rejection. "In the summer he is very busy, very important. In the winter he will do anything to turn a franc."

"I had a disagreement with my friend." I struggled to smile ingenuously. "I walked out on him. Do you know someone in town who would drive me?" I hesitated, searching for a figure. "For fifty francs?"

She smiled broadly.

"I am through here in twenty minutes. I can borrow a car and drive you there."

In the village, I paid off the waitress, hurried across the street to slide behind the wheel of the red compact—the upholstery, the wheel, hot from sitting hours in the broiling sun. Self-consciously, I glanced up and down the street. No sign of Neil. Had I honestly expected him to come back here and wait for me?

I cut out from the curb, braked with a jarring squeal because a dog chose that exact moment to saunter across the street directly in my path. A sprinkling of wine-drinkers watched me from the terrace café.

I squinted in thought. Neil had mentioned a public telephone just ahead, in a small shop. Go down there, try to phone Neil. *Apologize.*

My fingers were trembling as my mind tried to cope with the mechanics of a foreign pay phone. Eventually, I reached the *pension* where Neil was staying. He wasn't home. I was simultaneously disappointed and relieved. The confrontation was—at least—postponed.

I slid behind the wheel again, sat there in indecision. I couldn't keep buzzing him every twenty minutes. His landlady would be furious. Go back to the café, linger there over an ice? This turned me off.

Okay, drive back to the villa. Waste an hour in my room. How awful to waste time when I didn't know what was happening to Holly! Alone I felt frustratingly helpless. Neil gave me hope. Strength.

Could I find the house where he was staying? I dallied briefly over this possibility. No, don't try. The rebuff I'd

received when I asked directions to the villa still made me
flinch in restrospect. Drive back to the villa for an hour.

Frederic—looking like a teenage movie star in chinos
and summer tan—was on his haunches weeding a spectacular circle of blossoms as I drove up the driveway. He
glanced up timorously. Today he gathered the courage to
return my smile and wave.

I left the car in the garage, gave the key to Eduoard,
who had his head buried in the motor of a white Mer-
cedes. I could feel the weight of his gaze as I strode from
the garage. *I was so tired of contempt on every side.* Only
Helene—unfriendly at first in her maternal defense of
Frederic—was not hostile, of the whole domestic staff.

Opening the door to the villa, I momentarily froze, sensing instantly that I was walking into a moment of tension.

"Darling, you looked everywhere?" Stephanie was
asking solicitously. "Are you sure?" Her voice taut.

"Stephanie, I wore the bracelet to the casino last night."
Celia Whitney's voice was pitched unnaturally high. "I
had it on when I went up to my room. I remember it got
caught in the sleeve of my dress as I was pulling it off.
Jim, you remember!"

"Celia, you're so careless," her husband reproached her.
They were in the library, I mentally placed them while I
crossed to the stairs. "You must have stuck it away and
forgot where."

"I left it on that marvelous inlaid desk," Celia insisted.
"It was there when I went to sleep. I forgot about it until
now. Stephanie, what about the servants?"

"Celia!" Jim protested sharply.

"What about that American girl?" Celia demanded, and
my face burned as I started up the stairs. "That bracelet is
worth four thousand pounds."

"It's insured," her husband reminded dryly. "There's
no point in getting hysterical."

"We'll find it," Stephanie insisted. "We'll search everywhere."

I raced up the stairs to the privacy of my room. How

dare Celia Whitney suspect me! Oh, Holly and I would laugh about this later—when this nightmare was over.

I opened the door to my room, my eyes swinging spontaneously to the window. The broken panes had been replaced, the shattered glass swept away. Surprisingly, the bed was still unmade. Probably Celeste or Marie would be popping in any minute.

Without hearing the actual words, I was aware of the continued discussion downstairs about Celia's missing bracelet. Were they going to call in the police? The insurance people would probably send investigators if Celia Whitney phoned her broker to report the bracelet missing.

Should I go to the police about Holly? How can I let time roll by this way, with nothing happening? But what can the local police officer do? If I go to the Marseille police, they'll just list Holly as another "missing person." Somewhere in this segment of the south of France, Holly is being held under duress. *I have to find her myself.*

Neil will understand I was uptight, that I blew up that way from nerves. Won't he? I'll drive back into the village now. Try to reach him again. So his landlady will be angry. It's important that we ask everybody we see if they've encountered Holly. *Where is she? With whom?* Somebody will say something—some insignificant little thing—and suddenly we'll have a clue. *Oh, let her be all right.*

I hurried from the room, anxiously not to run into Celeste or Marie. Downstairs I cut through a side exit to the garage. In the library Jim Whitney was insisting that Celia wait until tomorrow to notify the insurance company that the bracelet was missing.

"Celia, you'll feel like an awful ass if the investigators pop in and you've found the bracelet stuck away somewhere."

No one was in the garage, for which I was grateful. I took my car key from the wall plaque, climbed behind the wheel, and drove out of the garage, down the driveway to the public road. Staring at, without seeing, the marvelous panorama of white sand, blue sea and sky.

I drove faster than normal. My heart pounded when I

spied the Renault pull up at the side of the road just ahead. Neil emerged from the car to signal me. I braked, cut off, the driver behind me cursing because he'd been tailgating.

"I've been searching all over for you." Neil chided gently while he crossed to my side of the road. "I figured it wouldn't be wise to call you at the villa," he reminded humorously.

"Neil, I'm sorry—"

"You little kook." He reached for my hand. "Hot-head." The pressure of his hand on mine was eloquent. Absurdly, I felt better.

"Neil, I'm so scared for Holly—"

"Don't fret," he exhorted. "Look. We'll start asking questions everywhere—of everybody we meet." He frowned in thought. "We'd better both drive into the village—we don't want to leave either car here. Follow me into town, then we'll make the rounds right there. It's too late to backtrack. You're still on that seven-thirty schedule?" I nodded. "Okay, let's head for the village."

I followed Neil into the small business area, parked directly behind him. Nobody here in town, I told myself, would go running to the villa to report we were seen together. Not the way the local people felt about the Manets.

With Holly's photos in hand, Neil and I went from one business place to another, asking if Holly had been seen. Our reception ranged from overtly hostile to coldly polite. Always the same answer: No.

With the area covered we left the village to head for the next one, keeping a sharp eye on the clock because I mustn't be late for dinner with Mme. Simone. Tonight the Manets' attorney—M. Rochambeau—was coming to the villa. It was to be an important meeting.

A mile out of town Neil pulled into a filling station for gas. Automatically he drew forth Holly's photos as he exchanged pleasantries with the unexpectedly friendly attendant, a slender man probably in his early fifties with a ruggedly lined face, meticulously trimmed grey beard, and somber eyes. His English was near-perfect.

"No, I have not seen the young lady." He gazed sharply at me. "You are staying at the Villa Fontaine, Mademoiselle?"

"Yes—" I was faintly disconcerted by the intensity of his stare.

"You are a friend of M. Jacques?"

"I've never met him." Did everybody in the village know I was staying at the villa? Which one of them had thrown that rock at me?

"Is your sister a friend of M. Jacques?" he persisted.

"Yes." My voice was a whisper. *What was he trying to find out?*

"His fiancée perhaps?"

"They are friends," I said stiffly, conscious of Neil's pantomimed warning to be uncommunicative.

"I have always felt affection for Jacques, because he is Paul's son. If Paul were alive, things would be different," he said bitterly. "His wife will bring ruin upon the village."

"Paul Manet was quite a hero in this town, wasn't he?" Neil asked gently.

The man straightened with pride.

"Paul and I fought side by side in the underground. For almost a year he was in a concentration camp. I was with him. He has a room laden with mementos of those days." His eyes wore the pain of memory. "Some of us will never forget the Occupation. Even now—all these years later—I hear the sounds of an ambulance racing through a city and I gasp—because it is like the siren on the Gestapo cars." He turned sternly to me. "Madame Manet is a selfish, evil woman. Do not stay in the villa. You will find only unhappiness there."

I was suddenly tense. Did he know about the rock? Did he know who threw it? Then he might be able to lead us to Holly and Jacques.

Not until we were in the car and well down the road did I question Neil about this.

"We won't get anything out of him," Neil rejected this possibility. "Not somebody schooled in the French Resistance. Only when he's ready to tell us. But we'll be around," Neil added reflectively. "I'll make a point of that."

In the next village we asked repeatedly for Holly—all the time watchful of the hour. We came up with nothing. Our brief encounter with Paul Manet's resistance companion gnawed at me. Our conversation replayed itself repeatedly in my mind. *Did he know something that would lead us to Holly?*

"We'd better call it a day," Neil decreed gently.

"I suppose," I admitted grudgingly.

"Tonight I'll buzz the magazine's Rome contact. I'll ask him to dig up the record of the marriage. The magazine won't use it, Janice," he reiterated. "You believe me, didn't you?"

"Yes." How could I have ever doubted Neil?

"Once I have a wire confirming the marriage, we'll go together to Stephanie. With the wire and your postcard. They'll prove to her that Holly and Jacques disappeared en route to the villa. We need the Manet money in this search, Janice—and the Manet power."

"I know—" My voice was uneven. I still suspected Stephanie's involvement in their disappearance. She didn't want Jacques at the villa. He might persuade Rochambeau to vote against the sale. "How fast will your contact in Rome work this out?" Jacques's office, my mind pinpointed. We'd contact them.

"He'll know in seventy-two hours. I'd guess," Neil said seriously.

"You'd think someone would have seen Holly and Jacques," I burst out with recurrent frustration. "How could they just disappear this way?"

"They may have been traveling at night," Neil offered. "Perhaps they say no one until—" Neil stopped short because he saw the anguish in my face. "Fifty miles away, possibly no one recognized Jacques," he reminded gently. "You know he has a hang-up about being photographed.

His office is supplying the photos for our magazine layout."

Neil went around the car to slide behind the wheel. I thought about the lack of photos about the villa. I had a towering curiosity to see my new brother-in-law. Holly's husband. Never did I have a doubt in mind that Holly and Jacques were married.

Neil drove me back to my rented car, then headed for a phone where he could call his Rome contact. I made a U-turn in the now-deserted street and headed back for the villa. Mme. Simone would expect me to dress for dinner.

Neil was right, of course. We desperately needed Stephanie Manet's backing in this search for Holly and Jacques. Let Neil's man in Rome come up quickly with the marriage records!

I drove the car into the garage, hurried into the villa. The stillness on the lower floor was broken only by the low hum of a vacuum cleaner somewhere to the rear. Helene was in the small sitting room off the foyer, replacing light bulbs in the wrought-iron wall sconces.

I walked quickly up the lushly carpeted stairs, down the corridor to my room, gearing myself for the tedious evening ahead, I wished there was some way I could phone Neil, ask if he'd reached the Rome contact.

I opened the door to my room. The bed was still unmade this late in the day. And then I saw her—a split-second before she saw me. Celeste. Standing by a far window. Fondling a diamond-encrusted bracelet that I knew, instinctively, belonged to Celia Whitney.

Celeste moved with spasmodic shock at the realization that I was in the room.

"Mademoiselle, look what I have found." Her eyes overbright, challenging. "I came in to do the room, and there it was on the floor."

"I believe that belongs to Mme. Whitney." I fought to appear casual. Celeste *hadn't* found it on the floor in my room. She had taken it from Celia Whitney's inlaid desk.

"I will take it downstairs." Celeste dropped the bracelet

into her apron pocket. A malicious aura about her smile. She was furious with me for walking in on her, for making it necessary to return the bracelet. "I will tell Madame I found it in the corridor."

I froze in shock as I realized her implication. Before I could verbalize my rage, she had stalked from the room, was headed at a swift gait for the stairs.

How dare she say she found the bracelet in my room! Suddenly I was trembling. And that condescension! Saying she would tell Stephanie she had found it in the corridor!

I crossed to the door, pulled it wide, moved towards the stairs. I spied Celeste and Helene, together in the foyer below, unaware of my presence.

"I found the diamond bracelet the English lady lost," Celeste was reporting. "I found it when I went in to do the American girl's room."

CHAPTER SEVEN

Ossified with shock, I hung there at the head of the stairs, Celeste's fabrication ricocheting in my mind. Helene and she moved into a room somewhere down the corridor. I could hear them talking with Stephanie, without being able to distinguish their words. My face stung with color as my imagination ran free.

"Thank you, Celeste." Stephanie was walking with them out into the corridor again. My throat was tight with rage. "I will give the bracelet to Mme. Whitney when she comes downstairs. She's lying down with a bad headache. I'm sure she will want to thank you personally."

I restrained myself from dashing straight downstairs and confronting Celeste in Stephanie's presence. That would be an ugly, melodramatic scene, but I couldn't *not* challenge that accusation of Celeste's. Oh, accusation it was!

I spun around, hurled myself back into the privacy of my room, feeling as all those innocent of crime but so accused must have felt through the centuries. Dress for dinner, I ordered myself. Stop off en route to Mme. Simone's suite and tell Stephanie Manet the truth. *Will she believe me?* Uneasily I recalled that Celia Whitney had asked about me. First the servants, than me. I was under suspicion.

My hands were shaking so that I had difficulty with the zipper down the back of the Pucci copy into which I had changed for dinner. I was impatient to be downstairs, to confront Stephanie. I ran a brush over my hair, touched a

71

lipstick to my mouth. Go downstairs. Tell Stephanie what happened.

I was breathless as I moved noiselessly over the lush, small Oriental rugs that formed an avenue down the marble corridor. I could hear Stephanie's talking in the small sitting room, the gathering place for pre-dinner cocktails, an American habit Stephanie enjoyed.

"Phil, now calm down," she was soothing. "These are stupid people."

"First they provide me with two flat tires, and then they smash eggs on both sides of the car!" A vein was distended furiously in Phil Carey's forehead. "What am I to expect next? And when I go to the local police officer, he shrugs his shoulders and shows no inclination to pursue the culprits!"

"Phil, I'm so sorry this has happened," Stephanie apologized. "But I'm sure there will be no other incidents. I'll have Robert take action. They have respect for him."

"Is Robert back?" Phil demanded.

"He'll be here for dinner. Perhaps in time for a drink," Stephanie's voice was persuasively charming. "Phil, there'll be no more incidents. I promise you."

"I'll go upstairs and dress for dinner," He seemed mildly mollified as I paused in the doorway. His eyes brightened as he spied me. "Ah, the mystery guest," he murmured. "Stephanie, you're naughty not to share her with us."

"Miss Carleton, my mother's companion," she introduced me. "This is Mr. Carey." Before we could pursue the conversation, Stephanie was walking him to the door.

"I'm sorry," I stammered when she came back into the room and turned inquiringly to me. "There's something I must talk with you about—"

"You've heard from your sister," she guessed, smiling brilliantly.

"No." How could I hear from Holly? She couldn't possibly know where I was. The realization hit a raw nerve. "It's about Mme. Whitney's bracelet." I forced myself to continue. Stephanie was suddenly bird-dog attentive. "I overheard Celeste tell Helene she found the bracelet in my room. That couldn't possibly be true. I walked into the room, and Celeste was standing by the window, the bracelet in her hand—"

"So that was it," Stephanie said quietly. I was grateful that she didn't appear surprised.

"Celeste was furious with me for walking in unexpectedly that way." I hesitated. "Perhaps she meant to keep the bracelet—I don't know. At any rate I couldn't let you think I had anything to do with it." Relief surged through me because, obviously, Stephanie realized I was telling the truth.

"I didn't check Celeste's references the way I should," Stephanie said wryly. "I had to hire help so unexpectedly—and it's so difficult to find people these day's. Particularly for just two weeks, this way. I'll pay her off tonight and dismiss her. I can't afford to have someone like that about the villa," She frowned in distaste. "Another incident like this and Celia Whitney will run right out. We could lose our business deal." Now she smiled warmly at me. "Thank you for telling me, Janice."

"Mademoiselle—" Helene's massive bulk dominated the doorway as I spun about, startled at being addressed. "Mademoiselle, I am sorry. Nicole has not timed herself properly tonight. Dinner will be served in five minutes in Mme. Simone's rooms."

"What is the matter with these people?" Stephanie flared, and shook her head in frustration. "We must make do for another week after this. Until the others return. Helene, tell Celeste she is to pack and leave. You will have to manage some way without her."

"*Oui*, Madame." Helene tried to mask her astonishment.

"I will give you two weeks' salary for her." Stephanie crossed to the desk, reached into a drawer, pulled forth a checkbook. "She doesn't deserve it—"

"I'll go to your mother's rooms," I told Stephanie quickly. Mme. Simone would be fretful if I didn't show right away.

"Janice, I hope you have some word from your sister," Stephanie said gently. "Have you notified anyone where you may be reached?"

"No, I haven't." I admitted. Again, unease infiltrated me. I hadn't considered thàt Holly would be in a position to call me.

"Put through a call to the States," Stephanie urged. "Consider it your expense account at the villa," she smiled. "Perhaps there will be some good word. There is a private line in the small sitting room. Helene, tell my mother that Mademoiselle will be with her shortly. Nicole can hold dinner ten minutes."

I told myself it was ridiculous to phone my building's superintendent back in New York. Yet I was uptight because Holly, of course, couldn't know that I was here. *Has Holly been trying to reach me?*

I waited impatiently for the call to be put through. The super and his wife knew Holly. She would have called them if she couldn't get through to me. Could there be a letter? A cable notice? Had I been behaving like an hysterical kook, running around over here this way? Oh, let it be that way! I didn't care how ridiculous I appeared if Holly was safe.

"Hello——" The Georgian-soft voice of my super's wife, faintly annoyed because I must have pulled her away from her TV set.

"Mrs. Meadows, this is Janice Carleton," I began.

"Oh, are you back home, Janice?" She knew I'd flown to France. I'd let her believe I was on vacation.

"No, I'm still in France," I said quickly and heard her gasp of astonishment. "I've missed connections with my sister. Did she try to reach me through you?"

"No."

"Could you check my mail and see if there's a letter from her?"

"While you wait on the phone?" She was aghast at the expense.

"Please," I urged. "I'll hold on."

"I'll be as quick as I can," she promised nervously.

I sat at the edge of the small, tapestry-covered chair, visualizing her sorting through the mail in the next room. The junk mail would be in the package room. Freddie would have automatically sorted this out. If there'd been a cable, Mrs. Meadows would already have mentioned it.

I waited, my throat tight with anxiety. If there was a letter, I'd ask Mrs. Meadows to open it, read it to me. *Could* I have been overreacting to this whole situation?

I heard Mrs. Meadow's elegant Siamese meow loudly.

"You just wait, Princess," she crooned, and then she was on the phone with me. "Janice, there's nothing from your sister," she reported. Her voice tense with the knowledge of what this call was costing. "No cable notice either. I hope you catch up with her soon."

"Thank you, Mrs. Meadows, I hope so."

Fleetingly, hope had welled in me. Now I was plunged into despair. Holly had not tried to reach me. I hadn't been overreacting. She was in desperate trouble.

I hurried to Mme. Simone's rooms. She was standing by a tall, narrow window that faced the deep red of the sunset over the Mediterranean. A sullen-faced Marie—I suspected she'd learned that Celeste was being ousted—was placing a paté, with thin wedges of toast, on the elegantly set table.

"The sunset's glorious, isn't it?" I said with defiant, phony high spirits. Marie shot an angry glance in my direction, blaming me for Celeste's early departure from the job.

"How are you, Janice?" Mme. Simone swung about with a vague smile. "Did you have a nice day?"

"Lovely," I lied.

"I'm just famished after my all-day fast."

Eagerly, Mme. Simone approached the table, entered into a lengthy monologue about her diet fads.

"The English don't know how to cook at all, you know," she said. "When I married M. Simone, I entered a whole new world gastronomically. Then—when Stephanie was a child—I met this doctor in Switzerland . . ."

I was relieved that I was required only to appear to listen, to make monosyllabic contributions at regular intervals. Why had I phoned home? My anxiety to find Holly was only intensified.

While Marie was ladling vichysoisse into the ornately painted soup plates which Mme. Simone fancied, we heard a car pull up before the villa. She stopped mid-sentence to leave the table and go check on the new arrival.

"That was Robert," she reported when Marie left us. "He isn't terribly rich but the family is one of the most influential in the south of France." She smiled archly. "One of these days Stephanie will give in and marry him, even though he is fifteen years older than she. Paul, too, was much older. Stephanie is drawn to older, important men." She preened with satisfaction. "Stephanie is beautiful, don't you think?"

"Yes, she is."

Stephanie could enlist M. Rochambeau's help in finding Holly and Jacques. Once he knew the facts—and saw a copy of the marriage license—he'd understand that Holly and Jacques were missing. Oh, let Neil's Rome contact work swiftly!

"My husband was handsome." Mme. Simone's eyes softened with sentiment. "Stephanie is very like him. She's not happy, though." She sighed heavily. "Not when her funds are so sharply curtailed. Jacques has these absurd ideas about business. Spoiling his employees so when they don't appreciate this at all. In France there's too much of this Communism," she said distastefully, then leaned forward anxiously. "Jacques is not a Communist—he's just being led around by the wrong people. Spending money foolishly. Why, Stephanie doesn't even go to the casino any more."

Dinner dragged on endlessly. Perhaps Nicole was punishing us because Celeste had been let go. There were depressingly long waits between courses despite Nicole's earlier announcement that dinner was ready ahead of schedule. Still, the veal was superb, the salad perfect. When dessert arrived, Mme. Simone was slightly mollified. Stephanie had ordered her favorite mousse.

"The French know how to cook," she said with a smile for Marie, who remained sullen. "Stephanie's guests are English, aren't they?"

"Yes." I sensed a wistfulness in her at being excluded from the socializing. Despite her constant reiteration that "my daughter is my whole life," Mme. Simone was lonely.

"I hope they appreciate the villa cuisine."

"I'm sure they do," I soothed. "I heard Mme. Whitney say she'd just adore to steal Nicole."

"Did you now?" Mme. Simone preened. "She can, you know. Nicole is here only while Michelle is on vacation." She frowned for a moment. "I don't know why Stephanie allowed the servants to go on vacation so early. She spoils them, like Jacques does. When is the English lady leaving?" A bare eagerness in her eyes now. With Celia Whitney gone, she would see more of Stephanie.

"As soon as the business is concluded," I soothed.

"Robert is so slow with everything," Mme. Simone complained. "This business—" She gestured vaguely. I doubted she knew the villa was up for sale. "The affair with Stephanie. If he pushed, she would marry him. He would do anything to make Stephanie happy."

Slightly past ten, Mme. Simone began to yawn.

"It's been a rough day for you," I murmured sympathetically, anticipating imminent escape. "All that fasting."

"I'll go to bed, sleep an hour—and then I'll lie awake forever," she forecast moodily. "I've decided the sleeping pills really aren't good for me. I promised myself this morning—while I was fasting—that I wouldn't take any more. The next time Stephanie and I go into Marseille, we'll stop by the English bookstore and pick up some mysteries."

"I have a couple with me." I rose to my feet. "I'll bring them down to you."

"Oh, that's a dear." She glowed. "If I can read, then the night won't be so long."

"It'll be only a few moments," I promised.

"I'll ask Marie to bring us hot chocolate," Mme. Simone decided, then frowned at the light knock on the door. "Come in," she called fretfully.

The door opened. Helene walked in, a glass in one hand, a small medicine bottle in the other.

"Your sleeping pill, Madame." Helene, terse and unsmiling, set the glass before her, unscrewed the top of the bottle.

"Not tonight, Helene."

"Madame, the doctor insists," Helene said firmly. "You are not to miss an evening."

"I don't want it!" Mme. Simone rebelled, but I knew from the wary glint in her eye that she expected defeat.

"Mme. Simone, let us not have another scene. You know you will take the pill in the end." Her eyes were eloquent as they seemed to mesmerize Mme. Simone.

"I will talk to the doctor when we go to him Friday." Grudgingly she accepted the pill. "I'll tell him I don't believe they're good for me. Helene," she added coldly when she had swallowed the pill beneath Helene's stern eyes, "tell Marie to bring hot chocolate for Mademoiselle and me."

"*Oui*, Madame." Helene stalked stolidly from the room.

"I'll run up for the mysteries." I was reconciled to lingering with Mme. Simone over hot chocolate.

"Come right down," she exhorted with an air of anticipation. "We'll have our little hot-chocolate party, then you can go up to bed."

I left Mme. Simone's rooms, crossed to the stairs. In the small sitting room, Stephanie and Celia Whitney were chatting with an air of brittle gaiety. The three men were closeted in the library.

"I told Jim to take care of that girl who found my bracelet," Celia was saying with curiosity. "He tells me she's gone."

"She received word about a sudden illness in the family," Stephanie fabricated. "But the help is all overpaid these days. Don't concern yourself about giving her money."

"I do hope we'll see Jacques this week," Celia said coquettishly. "That handsome man! I wish I were twenty years younger."

I moved somberly up the stairs to my room, my mind absorbed with Holly again. The man at the filling station had been so close to Jacques's father. We must confide in him, ask his help. Instinct told me this was right. The year of teaching had taught me to trust my instinct. Neil and I must talk with this man tomorrow morning.

I reached for the knob on the heavy oak door to my bedroom, assaulted now by the memory of last night. A chill wrapped itself around me as I remembered the shattered glass on the floor, the blood on my fingers from that minor cut that might have been major. Stephanie was so sure that rock was meant for her. My radar told me differently.

Nobody's going to try anything again. Last night was unpremeditated. A rock thrown in the heat of rage. *Nothing is going to happen tonight.*

But tonight the watchman Stephanie had promised would not be on duty. She'd told me they would send out a man for tomorrow night. I wished he would be here tonight!

I walked into darkness. Deliberately I crossed to draw the drapes snug against the night before I switched on a lamp. Tonight, no sitting duck, I promised myself grimly. I hesitated again before switching on a lamp. Make sure the windows are locked.

Now I dug out the two mysteries I'd packed in my valise, originally with the thought of reading them leisurely on the beach. Before this nightmare of Holly's disappearance.

The books in one arm—the lamp left on behind me—I went downstairs again. Marie had already brought the hot chocolate. Mme. Simone sipped dreamily, an odd smile on her face.

"Janice, how sweet of you," she welcomed me. "These two books will last me a week."

I sat down, reached for my hot chocolate, already poured for me.

"You don't have to worry about the hot chocolate," she whispered. "I made Marie taste it. It isn't poisoned."

She leaned back with a smile of satisfaction. I tried not to show that I was startled. She hardly seemed to be aware of my presence now as she sipped at the sweet, hot liquid. What was in that sleeping pill that Helene had given her? Was Mme. Simone being drugged at Stephanie's orders? *Why?*

I soaked in a perfumed tub for a luxurious twenty minutes, hoping wistfully to lessen the tension that imprisioned me. I started at each unexpected small sound—a rabbit hopping in the bushes below, a dog howling in the distance, a rumble of thunder. Were we going to have a summer storm?

After the tub, robe-wrapped against the night chill, I stretched across the bed and tried to concentrate on the French fashion magazine Mme. Simone had pressed upon me. But everything I saw reminded me of Holly. A pantsuit she would have liked. A piece of jewelry that reminded me of her period of designing in that field. A model posed before a Ferrari. In impatience I tossed the magazine aside.

Thunder again rolled through the sky. Ominous. On impulse I crossed to the window, opened a wedge between the drapes. Lightning crackled across the night sky, illuminating the choppy, dark sea below. I spied a ship coming into harbour. Down the shore red lights blinked on and off, calling other ships into port.

I drew my robe tightly about me. The approaching storm had brought about a sharp drop in temperature. A movement below, a sound, captured my attention. I peered curiously.

Stephanie was walking Robert Rochambeau to his black Citroën. Tall and slim, he would have been a rather handsome man except for that forbidding air about him.

Stephanie's arm was through his as they walked. Suddenly they stopped. Stephanie moved close, caught Robert by the shoulders, lifted her face to his. Guiltily I dropped the drapes, swung away from the windows.

I crossed to the fireplace, where cypress logs were piled high in readiness for a fire. For a few minutes I concentrated on the task of coaxing a blaze into being. The logs would smolder far into the night, spreading a colorful glow about the room. I'd welcome that glow.

In bed I pummeled the two pillows together, leaned back determined to sleep. Oh, set the alarm. I have to meet Neil at nine sharp. I must be back at the villa by one-thirty for lunch with Mme. Simone.

The alarm set, the lamp switched off, the logs in the fireplace wrapped in brilliant color, I lay back against the pillow, garnering comfort from the cheerfulness of the fireplace, the crackling of the logs.

Suddenly rain was pelting the villa, smacking the windows in a summer downpour that would soon spend itself. Downstairs someone moved about closing windows.

"Frederic, come inside!" Helene shouted somewhere below. "I do not want you out in this storm!" Frederic, taking childlike pleasure in the rain.

Resolutely I swung over on my side, burrowed my face against the mound of pillows. The steady beat of the rain was oddly mesmerizing. Assaulted by weariness, I closed my eyes.

I awoke with a startling suddenness, every nerve on alert. Rain hammered at the windows. The fire was completely obliterated when I'd expected the logs to smolder until dawn. A heaviness in the room made my heart pound. A labored breathing.

I was not alone.

I strained to penetrate the blackness. Somebody stood before the closet. Tall. Heavy. A man.

Trembling, I geared myself for action. What good would I be to Holly dead? I screamed. One frenzied, terrified scream. And with it I hurled myself over the far side of the bed to the protectiveness of the floor.

I lay there. Hearing the scurrying of heavy feet. My door opened and closed. I stumbled to my feet. Too late to catch a glimpse of the intruder. Why doesn't somebody run out and stop him? He's going to escape!

Now I heard the voices of those emerging from their rooms. Jim Whitney. Stephanie. Why didn't they stop him? He must be down at the front door by now.

"What is it?" Celia Whitney's voice was shrill. "What happened?

"Go back to your room, Celia," her husband ordered brusquely. "Stephanie, where did it come from?"

"Janice's room, I think," Stephanie said. "The American girl. The third door down."

"Stephanie?" Mme. Simone's voice came from below. "What's happening?"

"It's all right, Maman." Stephanie called down to her. "Stay there."

The man must have disappeared by now, I thought as I groped for the robe at the foot of my bed, pulled it on, fumbled for the switch on the bedside lamp. Someone was pounding urgently on the door.

"Miss Carleton! Miss Carleton!" Jim Whitney.

"Come in," I called out shakily.

The door swung wide. Stephanie darted forward, her face etched with anxiety. Jim Whitney trailed her. I could hear Mme. Simone climbing up the stairs as she talked to Celia. Mme. Simone was not supposed to climb stairs.

"Janice, what happened?" Stephanie demanded.

"I woke up and heard someone in my room." My voice sounded unnatural. "A man. I screamed and rolled over the side of the bed. He ran——" My voice petered out as my eyes focused on an object on the floor. Now I knew what he sought in the closet. A pillow lay on the floor where he had dropped it. Sick inside, I stared at the pillow. He had meant to smother me.

"Stephanie——" Celia's voice was laced with hysteria. "It

was someone after my jewels. He thought I was here in this room." She moved gingerly into my room, spied the pillow on the floor, shrieked. "Jim! I could have been murdered!"

"Celia, nobody's after your jewels," Stephanie soothed, trying to conceal her irritation at this outburst. "An intruder mistook Janice's room for mine." Again? "There're a few idiots in the village who don't wish to see us sell the villa. They meant to kill me." Her eyes were grim. She believed this.

"Celia, you'll take a sleeping pill and you'll feel fine in the morning," Jim said calmly.

"I don't have any sleeping pills," his wife pouted.

"I'll give you one of Maman's. Helene has them," Stephanie explained. Then Mme. Simone's sleeping pills could not be drugs, my mind registered subconsciously, She was truly "off."

"You all right?" Jim Whitney asked me with a searching gaze.

"Now I am," I said wryly. "A minute ago I was scared to death."

"Stephanie—" Mme. Simone hovered in the doorway, panting with exertion. "What happened?"

"Janice had a nightmare," Stephanie covered quickly. "She's all right, Maman."

"Madame—" Helene's voice echoed down the corridor. "Madame?"

"It's all right, Helene," Stephanie reassured her tiredly as Helene—in bulky robe and slippers—hurried into view. "Will you please take my mother back to her rooms? And bring Mme. Whitney one of Maman's sleeping pills, please."

"I went first to Frederic," Helene apologized. "These things frighten him." Now she turned to Mme. Simone. "Come, Madame. I will bring you hot milk to help you get back to sleep."

Phil Carey, scowling at his rude awakening, stood aside in the doorway to let Helene and Mme. Simone leave.

"What the devil's going on here?" He yawned broadly.

Succinctly Jim Whitney explained.

"Let's go downstairs and have a drink. We can all use one."

"You don't suppose he's somewhere around the villa yet?" I asked. Here was a link to Holly, my mind insisted —almost within my grasp for a moment.

"He wouldn't hang around," Carey said brusquely. "What about a drink?" His eyes moved about our small circle.

"None for me, thanks," I said quickly.

"Take Celia down to the library," Stephanie ordered the two men. "I want to see Janice settled in for the night. I'll be right down."

"I'm sorry I disturbed everyone," I apologized wryly when we were alone.

"It was that awful woman. Celeste." Stephanie frowned with distaste. She hadn't believed someone was after her—that was for Celia's benefit. "Because you reported her to me."

"It was a man," I reminded. A tall, heavy man. "I could see that in the dark." *The waiter at the café?*

"Celeste put him up to it," Stephanie insisted. "But how do we prove this?" She shook her head in frustration. "Tomorrow we must report this to the village *commissariat*." She searched my face. "Would you like me to stay with you for a while?"

"I'll be all right," I assured her.

"Good night, Janice."

I was in the room, shivering in the night chill. Or partly from the night chill. Start a fire again. It'll be something definite to do.

Now I realized why the room had been in darkness. While I slept, someone had banked the fire with ashes. Someone—that man—had stood right here by the fireplace and plotted my death!

Celeste had nothing to do with tonight's intrusion. There was one of two explanations for what happened. Either a villager—possibly the café waiter—hated me with such psychotic intensity that he wished me dead; or someone—knowing Neil and I had been asking questions in the village today—was fearful that we were getting close to Holly. Someone could be trying to stop me from searching for her. *Even if murder was the means.*

CHAPTER EIGHT

The night storm was past, dawn streaking the sky, by the time I fell asleep. I awoke before the alarm rang, reached over to stifle it's hour-distant message. The logs smoldered in the fireplace, providing a pleasant warmth in the unexpected chill of this morning.

I poked the logs into fresh activity, dressed before their heat, tired from the lack of sleep yet abnormally wide awake for this time of morning. Who was the man who had invaded my room last night? Someone we had questioned yesterday?

Tall, I inventoried as I reached into the closet for the beige suede jacket that would be comfortable over my pantsuit in this morning's coolness. *Heavy.* More than that I was unable to see in the darkness last night. Not one of the servants. Certainly not Frederic. Frederic—incapable of such an action, I was sure—was tall, but slenderly built.

I dug into my mind to try to pinpoint someone with whom Neil had talked yesterday. We'd questioned so many people. They formed a faceless glob in my memory. *It had to be somebody we questioned.* Because we were getting too close to Holly. I didn't believe Celeste was so furious with me she'd sent a man to kill me. That was illogical. Yet a killer was never logical.

Neil was going to be uptight when he heard about last night. It seemed as long since I'd said good-bye to him! He didn't even know about Celeste and the bracelet.

A shoulder bag slung over my shoulder, the suede jacket snugly buttoned against the unseasonable weather, I hurried down the stairs. The villa was wrapped in morning quietness. Stephanie and her guests would sleep late this morning after last night's disturbance.

What about the temporary staff, sleeping in rooms over the garage? They must have heard that one shrill scream last night. Humor brushed me gently. They must have heard me halfway down to the village. The servants had kept to their rooms. What had they thought when they heard me cry out that way?

As I reached the foyer I could hear Helene talking indignantly to someone at the rear of the downstairs floor.

"Leave the boy alone, Edouard! Do you hear me?" Her voice slashed through the quietness. "You are not to tease him!"

What did Helene think about last night? Did she know? Stephanie had offered no explanation last night in her anxiety to have Helene take charge of her mother. Even if Helene knew about the intruder, I doubted that she would confide in the other servants.

I cut through the side door, hurried through the crisp morning air to the garage. Frederic was mowing the lawn, concentrating on the small hand mower as though this were a major project. I slipped past without being noticed.

Well before nine I parked at the curb before the café. The village seemed deserted at this hour. The shops were closed. Only the restaurants showing signs of activity. A trio of tourists—I suspected they were Americans—were breakfasting on the café terrace. I sat at a corner table, waited a full ten minutes before a waiter appeared. I ordered a croissant and coffee, sat with my eyes fastened on the strip of road along which Neil would approach.

"Joe, how did you happen to know about this place?" One of the two women at the other table demanded avidly of their companion. "It's such a relief after all the resort towns."

"I took a wrong turn in the road," Joe said amiably. "Aren't you glad?"

If Stephanie's deal went through, this would be a tourist town next summer. Every table of the café would be jammed with patrons and the small shops cluttered with lookers—who might become buyers. Yet the village people rejected the prospective affluence. Remembering resort towns back home I couldn't blame them.

I squinted in the welcome sunlight. Was that Neil's Renault coming down the road? Yes. Suddenly I couldn't wait to spill out the story of last night's brush with death. I was trembling as I relived those terrifying moments.

The waiter—bringing my coffee and croissant—smiled knowingly as he watched Neil emerge from the Renault, stride towards my table. For the moment, I thought wryly, he was forgetting we were Americans.

"Have you been here long?" Neil slid into the chair across from me with a heartwarming smile.

"A few minutes," I fabricated. "I was impatient to get away from the villa this morning—" The tension in my voice reached through to him. Neil was staring sharply at me.

"Something happen?"

As concisely—as calmly—as I could, I reported the incident with Celeste, the intruder in my room, watching shock darken his eyes. I added my own convictions about the motivation for this unexpected visit.

"Two such things in a row have to have been plotted," he concurred. "I admit there was some doubt in my mind about the rock-throwing—it could have been meant for Stephanie. But now we know, Jannie. I think you ought to move out of the villa. It's too dangerous.

"Neil, no," I protested—knowing he was right. "I can't leave."

"You won't be any good to Holly dead," he pointed out grimly. "We'll drive around the nearby towns." He reached across the table to cover my hand with his. "We must find an off-the-beaten-track room for you. It won't be up to villa quality," he joked, "but I'll feel a lot better with you away from there."

"Neil, if anybody wants to track me down, he'll do it no matter where I am," I said intensely, then fell silent because the waiter was approaching to take Neil's order.

I shivered when I considered what any kind of room in

the resort area would cost me. Neil—on an expense account—could swing this. I didn't know how long I would have to stay here. I couldn't afford to take on the expense of living in one of the nearby towns.

"Neil, it's probably impossible to find a room this time of year," I pointed out. "Besides, I have to stay at the villa," I insisted, when we were alone again. "I have this kooky feeling that it's important for Holly's safety for me to stay."

"ESP?" he jeered gently.

"A hunch," I hedged. Plus the modesty of my supply of traveler's checks.

"Lock your windows and lock your door," he ordered. "*Can* you lock the door?"

"Yes." I'd locked it last night when Stephanie left me, feeling guilty. But somebody had walked into the night-garbed villa and into my room, with murderous intent.

"Janice, I don't like this." He frowned in rejection. "Whoever was in your room last night could try again. You ought to be on the next plane out of Marseille."

"Neil, I feel we're so close to finding Holly. I can't leave now." How could I leave when I didn't know where Holly was? How she was? "I'll be careful," I promised with a show of optimism I didn't feel. Inside I was terrified. For a long time I would remember that pillow lying on the floor.

"All right." Neil sighed, reaching into his jacket pocket to pull out a map. "I've marked the roads we've missed out. We'll start questions again. When must you be back at the villa?"

"One-thirty. I can clear out again by three."

"Okay. Let's have our coffee and get cracking."

With the map across my lap we followed the side roads Neil had marked. I looked at every barn, every farmhouse we passed with anguished suspicion. Could Holly be imprisioned there? How could we be sure we weren't driving right past her?

Could Holly be imprisioned at the villa? Suddenly my

throat was tight with excitement. Could Holly and Jacques be in the closed-off wing?

I must get into that wing! Say nothing to Neil about this. He'd consider it too dangerous. He'd be right—but I must take any chance that might lead to Holly.

"We'd better head back for the village," Neil decided finally, when we had stopped at endless farmhouses to make futile inquiries. "I'll meet you again about quarter past three. Okay?"

"Great." I lifted my face to his with an apologetic smile. "What a way for you to spend your time on the glamorous Côte d'Azur!"

"I don't know any better way to spend it," he said quietly, "than with you."

With only a disinterested cow for an audience, Neil pulled me into his arms and kissed me. For a few exquisite moments I could forget my anxiety about Holly.

"A miracle, the way we met," Neil whispered. "We could have spent the rest of our lives in New York without meeting."

Later, I promised myself, we'd laugh and say Holly deliberately got into a scrape so that Neil and I could meet. And she would say that our meeting was destined. *What was destined for Holly?* A coldness swept about me as I considered this.

Hand in hand Neil and I returned to the Renault. Knowing Neil was here—that he would see me through this awful time—gave me the strength to return to the villa.

"Neil, the man at the filling station yesterday—"

Neil was instantly attentive.

"What about him?

"I have this feeling that we ought to go back and talk to him. No reason," I admitted. "Just instinct."

"I trust your instinct." He reached to turn the ignition key. "I gave him a thought last night, too. Let's drop by and buy some gas this afternoon. The proprietor may be in a garrulous mood."

We drove back to the village in a comforting silence.

Once Neil's hand left the wheel briefly to squeeze mine in encouragement. I dropped my head on his shoulder at his invitation. When this nightmare was over, there would be time for us. Holly, with that positive warmth of hers, would adore Neil.

We parked in the village. Neil walked with me to my car.

"If I have a cable tomorrow, confirming Holly's marriage to Jacques," he said seriously, "Stephanie ought to be shaken up to the point of calling for help. With luck we may have the whole Manet organization in action."

"Oh, Neil, if we only could!"

Despite the ogling couple watching us from a café table, Neil leaned forward to brush his mouth against mine. Could it be that I'd known Neil only since Tuesday? It seemed months!

When I pulled up before the villa—parking out front because I'd be leaving immediately after lunch—I spied the modest police car that sat directly ahead. Stephanie had brought in the police despite her contempt for the local law-enforcement capabilities. My heart thumped uncomfortably. There would be all kinds of questions ahead.

Self consciously, I left the car, walked up the stairs to the entrance. How much did I admit about Holly's disappearance? Everybody in the villlage *knew* I was looking for her. Could the policeman inside help Neil and me?

I hear Stephanie in the library, her voice crackling with that imperious quality she used when talking with the servants.

"How do I know how the man got into the house?" Stephanie challenged scornfully. "An intruder makes his own ways. He came into the girl's room and he would have smothered her with that pillow if she had not awakened and screamed."

"Where is the girl?" the policeman was inquiring with a note of reproof. "Why is she not here?"

"She drove into town." Robert Rochambeau was studiously detached. "There was no need for her to be confined to the villa."

I quickened my pace down the corridor.

"I'm here," I called out casually.

I paused in the doorway, suddenly breathless. A short, heavily mustached policeman who obviously took his job with utmost seriousness was scribbling into a notebook. Stephanie—dark eyes kindled with annoyance—rested against an edge of the desk. The impeccably tailored Robert Rochambeau—this was the first occasion on which I encountered him face to face—sat in a black leather chair, his legs crossed, his distinguished face touched with a tolerant smile. I could visualize him in court, pleading his case with deadly understatement.

"Mademoiselle." The policeman nodded curtly. "You will please answer some questions."

M. Rochambeau pantomimed for me to sit in the chair beside his own, his eyes revealing mild amusement at the officiousness of our policeman. I sat back, trying to concentrate on the questions that were shot at me. This was like the script for a D movie.

When I tried to tell him that I had come to the south of France to search for Holly, he dismissed this impatiently. I was to confine myself to answering his questions. I recoiled from his officiousness.

"Do you think you can catch the man?" Stephanie interrupted impatiently because my interrogator was probing into my personal background, though he refused to let me tell him about Holly. What did it matter that I taught French in a junior high back in the States? "Monsieur, my guests are quite disturbed."

The policeman stared coldly at her.

"This time of year, Madame, the village sees many tourists passing through. Some of these people are bad. I am one man. I cannot follow them all."

From the hostility in his eyes I guessed he was contemplating next summer's tourist invasion should the resort be ready. But he snapped his notebook shut—out of respect for Rochambeau, who practiced law in Marseille.

"The intruder was a thief. The pillow was a defense weapon. He did not use it," the policeman pointed out with malicious triumph. "When Mademoiselle awoke, he ran." His eyes moved from one of the other of us. "No one saw this man?" he tried again. "Mademoiselle screams and nobody runs out to check?"

"By the time we awoke and emerged from our rooms, he had fled," Stephanie reminded. "We were all groggy from sleep, upset—"

"I will do the best I can," the policeman said formally. "You have given me little." *What about Holly?* He must know. Couldn't he realize the intruder was out for murder, not for theft? No, this man would be of little use to Neil and me if he couldn't see the implications right before him.

"We have a night watchman arriving this evening," Rochambeau reported crisply. He rose to his feet. "I trust there will be no repetitions of last night."

"I trust not." The policeman flushed slightly in resentment of the attorney's dismissal. "*A urevoir,* Madame, Mademoiselle, Monsieur—"

"He'll do nothing, of course," Stephanie said quite softly while the policeman stalked heavy-footedly down the corridor to the door. "But Celia will feel more comfortable because we've reported the incident."

"She'll feel more comfortable with the watchman parading the grounds," Rochambeau said dryly. "From sundown to sun-up."

"It was that stupid maid," Stephanie said insistently. "It had to be."

"We don't know who it was," Rochambeau corrected matter-of-factly. "As he said, there are many tourists passing through town during the summer months. The villa indicates wealth to these people."

All at once I felt discomfited because Robert Rochambeau was gazing fixedly at me. I guessed he shared the local contempt for tourists. Stephanie had told him that I was here as a part-time temporary companion to her mother. I was disconcerted by the displeasure I sensed in him. He thought I was riding free here at the villa, using Stephanie for a free vacation.

"Excuse me." I rose to my feet with a defensive smile. "Mme. Simone will be expecting me to join her for lunch."

"When will the girl be leaving?" His voice filtered out to me before Stephanie closed the door. "First the rock thrown through the window, now this business last night. She is not being honest with you, Stephanie—" Why hadn't Stephanie told him why I was here? I was sure she had said nothing about my insistence that Jacques and Holly were married.

Mme. Simone was in her sitting room, staring at a page of a magazine. The table was laid for luncheon.

"It's a lovely day," I said brightly. "Cool as early autumn."

"Yes it would be a nice day for a little drive to Marseille," she said regretfully.

"If tomorrow morning is this lovely, why don't you tell Marie at breakfast to set up the luncheon table on the terrace?" I coaxed. "You'll enjoy that."

Mme. Simone's face lighted. She nodded vigorously in approval as she rang for Marie to serve. Her whole life was a mosaic of the insignificant.

Marie served us elegantly broiled filet of sole, string beans with almonds, a salad prepared from greens grown at the villa. Her face sullen as she moved about the table. Marie, like the other servants, had not left her room over the garage last night, I recalled. What did they think? *What did they know?*

Over the mousse and coffee, I concocted the plot that had been simmering in my mind all morning. A way to gain access into the closed-off wing.

"Is the other wing of the villa," I asked Mme. Simone with an ingenuous smile, "as lovely as the part being used?"

"Oh yes," She preened with pride. "The furniture there is priceless."

"In what period is it furnished. "I made a show of admiring curiosity.

"Oh, I don't know about those things." She gestured vaguely. "But it goes back centuries. It required so much attention that Stephanie decided it best to close off the whole wing. You know the domestic problem these days." She sighed delicately, her eyes on the door. I sought frenziedly for a leading question, but she anticipated me. "Would you like to see it?" She smiled like a small child on the point of embarking on forbidden adventure.

"I'd love to." My heart was pounding. The others were in the dining room. Could we enter the closed-off wing without Stephanie's knowledge? "I'm fascinated by antiques."

"We'll go as soon as we've finished our coffee."

I struggled to conceal my impatience to explore that closed-off wing. I'd be avidly curious. Insist on peering behind every door. If Holly and Jacques were imprisioned in that wing, I'd find them.

En route to the closed-off wing, Mme. Simone—reveling in her role as guide—led me to a room at the turn of the corridor.

"This is Paul's memento room," she explained, and I remembered the man at the filling station telling us about this. "We'll stop in for a visit."

She reached for the knob of the ornate oak door, opened it, gestured me inside while she found the wall switch.

The floor was thickly carpeted in an earth-colored wool. One stark white wall was adorned with framed newspaper clippings that dealt with the exploits of Paul Manet and his Resistance group. Shelves on the other walls displayed guns, grenades, radio sets, the various instruments of the underground operations. A printing press stood in one corner. On a small table at its side was a stack of bulletins, printed just prior to the liberation.

I felt as though I had stepped into a page of history. For Paul Manet and the man at the filling station these years had never been forgotten.

"Come," Mme. Simone prodded me gently. "Let us go into the other wing. Stephanie is busy with her guests," she said with a conspiratorial smile. "She won't know."

A door down a corridor to our left led us into the unused wing. Mme. Simone found a wall switch that provided us with illumination. The windows of these rooms were boarded up against the outdoors; the furniture was draped with cloths. As we moved from room to room, she pulled aside the cloth from special pieces to show them off to me.

This closed-off wing consisted of one floor, a myriad of rooms of what I believed to be varying periods. But nowhere any sign of Holly and Jacques. Reluctantly—at last—I conceded this had been a futile foray.

"We will have another cup of coffee," Mme. Simone decided when we had returned to the main wing of the villa. "I'll ring for Marie. She'll still be in the kitchen."

We settled ourselves in Mme. Simone's sitting room. The table had been cleared away in our absence. Marie appeared in answer to Mme. Simone's summons—sullen at this fresh demand for service, but quick to comply.

"Do you often have nightmares, Janice?"

"Never," I began emphatically, and hastily caught myself. "Except for last night—"

"You're worried about something, my dear," she declared with dramatic sympathy. "Can you tell me? Sometimes it helps just to talk."

I hesitated. How could Mme. Simone help me?

"I'm worried about my sister Holly. I came to the village to meet her—" I couldn't say Holly was supposed to be here at the villa. "I couldn't locate her—I've asked everywhere around."

"Did you go to the American Embassy in Marseille? The Embassy people are always charming."

"Holly would be just another missing American. They get hundreds of such cases every summer. And Holly wasn't coming from Marseille. She was driving from Rome."

"Go into the village," Mme. Simone urged. "Ask for di-

rections for the filling station of M. Ferney. Charles Ferney knows everything that happens in these parts, Jacques
always says. Ask him to help you find your sister."

CHAPTER NINE

Neil was standing beside the Renault, engrossed in the international *Herald Tribune*. I honked lightly and pulled off to park. Neil folded over the newspaper, stuffed it into his jacket pocket, strode across the narrow street to me.

"What's happening in the outside world?" It felt so reassuring to be with Neil.

"Usual earth-shattering problems." He smiled, reached for the car door. "Janice, I spoke with our man in Rome an hour ago— "

"What did he say?" My heart thumped like a conga drum in action as I stepped from the car.

"Nothing concrete," he cautioned. "He's still checking registry offices for a marriage license. But he's picked up word that Jacques was definitely in Rome ten days ago."

"When Holly was there!"

"He was seen about town with a blonde movie starlet— "

"Holly was playing a bit part in a low-budget film," I said bluntly, my excitement ebbing.

"Honey, in Rome every beautiful American girl is a movie starlet. The Italians are romanticists. The girl was Holly," he said emphatically, and grinned. "My instinct tells me. Come on. Let's get into the Renault and go ask more questions."

Not until we were in the Renault and Neil was pulling that much-handled local map from the glove compartment did I mention what Mme. Simone had said to me.

"The Charles Ferney she was talking about must be the man we spoke with at the filling station."

"Okay." Neil nodded in agreement. "Let's go buy some gas."

There was a garrulous customer ahead of us. I reined in my impatience as we sat in the car and waited. Neil was turned on at our pinning Jacques in Rome ten days ago. He was anxious now for action.

"As many liters as she will take," Neil told our friend when he walked over to our car. "You're M. Ferney, aren't you?"

"Yes." He squinted cautiously at us. We hadn't bothered to inquire about his name yesterday.

"Mme. Simone at the villa suggested we talk to you," I confided on impulse. "She says you know everything that goes on in the village. Jacques told her that," I amended.

His smile was noncommittal.

"I have lived long in the village. My parents and my grandparents lived here. I know many people." He deliberated a moment. "Come inside. We will talk."

The inner office was tiny. A desk and two chairs filled it. He gestured Neil and me to the chairs, thrust aside a pile of newspapers to settle himself at a corner of the desk.

"The girl whose photo we showed you yesterday," Neil began carefully. "Jacques's fiancée." Yesterday I had labeled them friends. Did Ferney *know* they were married? Had Edouard told him that I claimed this? "They were en route from Rome to the villa. They never arrived."

"Have you told this to Stephanie?" he asked sharply.

"Stephanie doesn't know about Holly and Jacques. She's certain he's off on some research project. But I had a letter from my sister in Rome. She told she was going to the villa with Jacques. Then I received a postcard—it was postmarked fifty miles from here." I mentioned the town and he nodded somberly, attentive now. "They were going to stay there overnight, drive to the villa in the morning. *They never arrived.*"

"What does Stephanie have to say about this? You must have discussed it."

"Stephanie is positive Holly is with someone masquerading as Jacques. She is convinced Jacques is tied up in business. She expects him here momentarily. *He won't be.*"

"Then Stephanie will be concerned," he pinpointed realistically.

"No," I rejected. "Jacques has a reputation for disappearing from view when he's involved with his work. Stephanie will think he's only delaying again. And all the while Holly and Jacques are in terrible danger." I didn't allow myself to think what might have already happened to them.

"Twice now attempts have been made on Janice's life," Neil said.

"Why?" Ferney demanded.

"Because she's searching for Holly and Jacques. Somebody's terrified she'll stumble on to their whereabouts."

"What kind of attempts?" Ferney was bird-dog attentive. "Are you sure about these?"

Neil succinctly explained. Ferney listened impassively. I didn't know if he were impressed or not.

"Why did you come to me?" He reached for his pipe, occupied himself with the small business of stuffing aromatic tobacco into its bowl.

"Because you are a friend of Jacques's father," I reminded earnestly. "Because you feel affection for Jacques."

"What can I do?" Suddenly he was explosive. "We cannot go into every house and search for them. Perhaps they are not missing at all. Perhaps they have gone somewhere to be alone together."

"No!" I shot back. "My sister told me twice—once in a letter from Rome and once via the postcard—that she would be at the villa on Friday. Last Friday." I was trembling now. A *week.* An unaccounted-for week in Holly's life. "Holly would never say this unless she meant to be there."

"Stephanie has not talked with Jacques? You are sure of this?"

"She admits it," Neil said, the only calm one among us. "She simply can't see the element of danger."

"What is going on at the villa?" Ferney asked. "The English people are still there. Is it as the villagers fear, that the English syndicate is buying?"

"Rochambeau is drawing up the contracts," I confirmed. I must trust Charles Ferney. "Of course, something could throw it off at the last moment. Stephanie is very nervous."

"Why is Jacques allowing her to do this? He knows what will happen here. He made such promises to the villagers!"

"Find Jacques," Neil urged quietly. "Perhaps you can convince him to stop this sale."

"They came before and Jacques sent them away. Why is he letting Stephanie go through with it now?" Ferney rose to his feet, shook his head impatiently.

"The money has been doubled," I reported. Guilty at repeating what I'd overheard. "There's the financing for the plant."

"Not at the cost of the village!" Ferney shot back. "Do you know what it will be like here if the villa becomes a resort complex? The village will be overrun with tourists. Business people will flock in from the cities to open up their fancy shops and restaurants and bars. Our streets will stink of gas and expensive perfumes. Our beach will be polluted, noisy with the screech of motorboats and water-skiers. The village will be swallowed up." A vein throbbed in his forehead. His eyes were brilliant with contempt.

"Do you know the terms of M. Manet's will?" Neil asked.

"Vaguely," Ferney said. "If there is a question of a sale, and Jacques and Stephanie disagree, M. Rochambeau has the deciding vote." His voice was dry. "M. Rochambeau's integrity is unquestioned here, but he has long been in love with Stephanie. Obviously she has persuaded him to side with her."

"If we can find Jacques, you can talk to him," Neil pushed. "Convince him to talk to Rochambeau. Change the attorney's mind on this!"

"I?" His chuckle was bitter. "I am a stranger these days at the villa. The first year of Paul's marriage I was at the villa four times for dinner. After that, never. Paul came to me. For Stephanie and the attorney the Resistance companion was not a social equal. I have lived alone since my wife died fourteen years ago. In my little house by the sea. Down there." He pointed towards a small beach cottage. "My three children are married. They left the village. What is there here for them except the fishing? On that they cannot make a living. The young run. Sometimes they come back. For a while we hoped that the plant Jacques had proposed to build would provide jobs for them." He paused to light his pipe. "I will ask if anyone knows about Jacques or the girl. If they have been seen, I will know." He turned to Neil. "Where can you be reached?"

Neil and I drove back onto the road again, heading away from the village.

"Ferney will take care of the people in his area," Neil pointed out gently. "Let's take the side road towards Hyères. Ask around there. If we can pinpoint a specific locale," he said with recurrent frustration, "we could concentrate a search in that area. I sound like a bad TV script, don't I?"

"Nobody else is searching for them," I reminded defiantly. I was prepared to crawl through the dark into barns and cellars if need be. "Except for Charles Ferney," I amended. "He's concerned." That was fine because he was stirred into action. Yet his concern confirmed all my fears for Holly's safety.

"I received that message, too. Ferney will go all out to help." Neil removed a hand from the wheel to brush mine reassuringly. "Feel like stopping for coffee? There's a place just ahead."

"Let's stop," I agreed. The back of my neck, my shoulder blades ached with tension. I needed to sit down over coffee and try to unwind. It touched me that Neil recognized this.

We pulled off the road before a small, weathered café with three outdoor tables, all unoccupied. A buxom, smiling waitress moved eagerly towards us as we approached a table. How different from the waiter at the village café!

"Coffee and pastries," Neil decided casually.

"Just coffee for me," I said, remembering that sumptuous lunch with the coffee mousse.

"You want to insult them?" He clucked reproachfully. "Coffee and pastries," he ordered, and the waitress hurried off with a broad grin for Neil's college French. For a little while we were just a pair of American tourists.

The waitress returned, held forth a tempting tray of pastries, all of them enticing. We made a production of choosing, with our waitress beaming at our pleasure.

"Now how could you have considered turning down this?" Neil jibed when the waitress had deftly transferred pastries to plates and returned to the kitchen for our coffee.

"It's a good feeling not to feel like an intruder," I said whimsically. "These people don't hate tourists."

"It's not the same situation as back in the village," Neil reminded, serious again. "They're not living on the brink of a heavy tourist invasion. They're grateful for the dollars a few tourists—even Americans—bring in during the summer. Of course, in the cities there's little liking for the American tourists—though they grab fast enough for the American buck. It was kind of a shock to me at first. Americans grow up with the certainty that the whole world is going to like them."

"A couple of the teachers back at the school who'd been over for three weeks last summer warned me the prices in the restaurants could be wild. They said, 'Don't go in even for a cup of coffee without reading the menu on the window first!' "

Neil chuckled.

"You can spend most of your sightseeing time searching for inexpensive places to eat. You see a lot of disenchantment these days."

"At Orly I paid a dollar for coffee and a croissant," I recalled.

"In Copenhagen—magnificent Copenhagen," he said nostalgically, "I paid two dollars for scrambled eggs and tea in what's supposed to be an inexpensive restaurant. Stockholm was even worse. Wherever you go in Europe—in the *cities*," he emphasized, "you find inflation taking over. Geneva, Paris, Rome—the same situation. You can eat less expensively in London, but the food!" He shuddered in retrospect. "And even London isn't the budgeteer's paradise it was four years ago, the first time I came over. Yet you go out of the cities into the villages and you can eat fabulously—and what portions!—for what you'd pay at a Horn & Hardart back home."

Neil talked animatedly about his excursions into Europe for the magazine. He loved people. He enjoyed talking with them, mentally dissecting them, filing them away in the back of his mind for future use.

"I don't intend to stay with the magazine forever," he said quietly while the waitress filled our cups again. "Someday I want to write seriously. Not now. I don't know enough."

"About writing?"

"About people. Life—" He gestured broadly. "Someday I'll write about the fourteen months in Vietnam. Not now," he said quickly. "Later, when I can look back and see it all the way it acutally was. I was lucky to get out. I got this bug, and the doctors didn't know how to handle it. So I got shipped home." His eyes were bitter for a moment. "In one piece—for which my mother nightly thanks God."

We finished our coffee and started out again. We couldn't cover much more ground today. At a fork in the road Neil slowed down.

"Which way?" Neil asked. "Any hunches?" His eyes tender, mocking gently at my inclination to follow instinct.

I hesitated, my heart pounding. Every time there was a decision such as this to be made, I felt a tremor of excitement because one way might lead us to Holly.

"To the left," I decided. And was instantly assailed by doubt. "The left," I reinforced, thrusting out doubt.

We swung left, traveled along a road of isolated farms, stopping at each house to make our inquiries, encountering a succession of negative replies. Three miles down the road the car suddenly wobbled. Neil swore.

"A flat," he sighed. "Okay, I might as well get out and change it."

We both left the car, viewed the flat—the right front tire—with impatience. I followed Neil to the trunk, where he pulled out the spare, then searched with soaring frustration for the jack.

"No jack," he conceded unhappily. "I ought to sign myself in for a sanity test. How could I rent a car without checking for the triangle, the green insurance card, and the jack? My brother Ted—who worked for Standard Oil in Paris for four years—drummed that into my head the first time I had to rent a car in Europe!"

"So you goofed once," I consoled him. "It happens."

"We'll walk down to the next house, ask if we can borrow a jack or phone a garage," he decided, then grinned. "Did you check your car for the triangle, the insurance card, and the jack?"

"I didn't think of it," I confessed. "When I picked up the car in Marseille, I wasn't thinking of anything except how fast could I get to the villa."

"Know what you're paying for car rental?" he demanded, shutting the trunk with an unnecessarily heavy hand.

"That I know." I nodded grimly. "And for an automatic the price jumps so high. But I wouldn't have dared try to drive a manual."

"You don't know you're paying by the kilometer, do you? Rather than the mile?" he challenged.

"I hadn't thought of that." I'd been too uptight, back there at the car rental office, to calculate the difference.

"A kilometer is five-eighths of a mile," Neil reminded, and I grimaced. "So your rental over here is going to run high in American dollars." He reached for my hand.

"Come on, let's do some hiking. I'll give you a crash course while we walk on how to survive as an American tourist in Europe."

The woman at the farmhouse had no jack. She had no telephone, she explained matter-of-factly. But there was a garage about a kilometer down. She walked out onto the porch with us to indicate the direction.

"*Allez tout droite*," she instructed firmly, pointing.

The garage was a freshly painted white outbuilding at the side of the road. Only cars were in view as we approached.

"Anybody home?" Neil called out blithely in French.

A face emerged from beneath a creased-hooded Citroën.

"A moment, Monsieur."

In grease-smeared coveralls he pulled himself out from beneath the car—a small, compactly built machine with a ready smile.

"We're about a kilometer down the road," Neil explained. "With a flat and no jack. Can you change the tire for us?"

"Not now, Monsieur," he apologized. "A man comes soon for this—" He pointed to the Citroën. "But I will be happy to loan you a jack." His smile was warm. His eyes were admiring as they rested on me. Neil noticed, grinned. "Take the truck there—" He pointed to a vintage pick-up. "So you do not have to walk. The keys are in the ignition."

"Thank you," Neil accepted with relish.

In the truck we headed back to the car.

"A Frenchman always has an eye for a beautiful girl and a fine bottle of wine," he drawled. "You made a conquest back there."

"What comes first?" I joked. "A bottle of Romandée-Conti or me?"

Neil changed the flat. I slid behind the wheel of the Renault to follow Neil in the truck. My eyes scanned each farmhouse we passed, the inevitable question plaguing me. *Where was Holly?*

Neil drove the truck into the parking area before the garage. I drew up beside him. On impulse I emerged from the car, trailed Neil. He was thanking the mechanic for the use of the jack and the truck. A note passed from Neil's hand to the mechanic's.

"Neil, show him Holly's photos," I said in English. A sudden excitement took hold of me.

Neil glanced sharply at me for an instant, reached into his jacket pocket to bring out the two wallet photos.

"Have you seen this girl around the area?" Neil asked casually. "Sometime in the past week or so? She's Janice's sister—they've missed connections."

The mechanic leaned over to inspect the photos, not wanting to touch them with his greasy hands.

"Yes," he said definitely, and my heart pounded. "They stopped for water. Their engine was overheated. What a car!" He gestured expressively.

"What kind of a car?" Neil probed.

"A Ferrari. A red Ferrari."

"Did you know the man with her?" I asked, my throat tight. Holly had been here! "Was he someone from around this area?" Even this far from the village Jacques should be recognized.

"I am sorry, Mademoiselle," he apologized. "I bought the garage only a short time ago. I have moved from Avignon. I know few people here."

"But you're positive you saw this girl?" Neil probed. "In a red Ferrari?"

It had to be Holly. She'd said they were driving a red Ferrari. Her wedding present.

"Oh, the Mademoiselle I could not forget." He kissed his fingers ecstatically. *"Très belle."*

CHAPTER TEN

"What do we do now?" Trembling, I settled myself on the front seat of the Renault beside Neil.

"It's important to establish that Jacques was with Holly," Neil said slowly, "if we're to convince Stephanie that action's necessary. We'll have to show the man a photo of Jacques."

"If I could only get a photo out of the villa!" I exclaimed in frustration. "I haven't seen one around." Admittedly, I was curious about my new brother-in-law.

"Jannie, I told you—he's camera-shy." Neil chuckled. "I gather it's a hang-up that remains from childhood. He was a pudgy kid who loathed being photographed."

"Neil, there must be some photographs in existence."

"Occasionally, some candid shots—not good ones— have appeared in magazines." He squinted in concentration. "I saw a couple in a French movie-magazine layout several weeks ago, when we first started talking about this article."

"Can we get copies of them somewhere?" It would take too long to ask for them to be mailed from the magazine office. "Perhaps in Marseille?"

"Yes." Neil's voice was laced with resolution. "We'll hunt down a second-hand-magazine shop in Marseille. We might—with luck—come up with something." He checked his watch. "Want to take a chance on driving with me to Marseille? It's a fast run on the autoroute. If we don't waste time in the city, I should get you back before seven-thirty."

I hesitated, reluctant to show up late at the villa. But I

109

must go with Neil. He'd need help in skimming through what might be tons of old magazines.

"I'll come with you, Neil—"

We stopped at the side of the road to examine Neil's road map.

"We cut north here." Neil pointed, indicating a side road. "It takes us directly to the autoroute. Not as picturesque as the road along the sea, but we'll make time."

In several minutes we'd left behind us the quiet country road and were on the impressive autoroute which would take us directly to Marseille.

"How much did you see of Marseille?" Neil asked. My eyes gaped at the speedometer reading until I realized this was a hundred twenty kilometers rather than miles.

"Only La Canebière. First from the back seat of the taxi that took me to the car-rental agency, and then from behind the wheel. I wasn't exactly in a sightseeing mood," I acknowledged.

"Marseille is the oldest city in France. It goes back twenty-five centuries. It's also the second largest. Did you know the port was completely artificial?"

"No." I was astonished.

"The port complex is enormous. It services ships from Africa, the Middle and Far East, South America, and the Pacific islands. Once this is all over, Jannie—and before we head back for New York—we must take a day and go aboard some of the international liners. They allow you to do that."

When this was all over. *When?* My momentary sense of wellbeing fizzed away again. My eyes clung to the ribbon of road ahead. If we could prove—via a witness—that Jacques and Holly had been eleven miles from the village, *together,* Stephanie must throw all her efforts into the search to find them. Perhaps this concrete proof would prod Charles Ferney into even greater action.

Sooner than I'd dared to expect we saw the city of Marseille rising before us.

"We cut off just beyond," Neil said when we were skirting the city to the north. "The cut-off takes us into La Canebière."

We rode along the upper, tree-planted La Canebière at the height of the afternoon traffic, Neil swearing softly at the delays. Now I took time to inspect the magnificent avenue with its sumptuous shops, the cafés with their crowded terraces, the elegant hotels—noticing, as I had not on my earlier trek down this avenue, the predominance of sailors of all nations, declaring Marseille one of the great seaports of the world.

At the first opportunity Neil turned off and sought a parking spot.

"Worse than New York," he grumbled. "As bad as Paris or Rome or Geneva."

"Somebody's pulling out just ahead, Neil—"

Neil braked, waited to slide into the barely adequate wedge, ignoring the honking horns behind us. The car at the curb, we left, sidetracked into a tobacco shop to ask questions. Yes, there was a second-hand bookstore just four blocks away. The proprietor shrugged when Neil asked if the shop handled magazines.

"Je ne sais pas, Monsieur."

We sought out the bookstore, its small quarters jammed with tables, the aisles a hazard for anyone of impressive girth. A question elicited the information that the magazines were below.

We made our way down the narrow stairs to a cellar equally cluttered. Neil spied a table piled high with movie magazines.

"All those?" It seemed incredible that so many existed. The stacks were formidable, towering precariously above the table. How could we ever search through them all?

"Start looking," Neil ordered, apprehensive as he tackled one corner. "Oh, the recent issues are over here."

For me it was more difficult than for Neil. He sought a face. I must read the names. Impatiently I flipped through the first magazine, nervous that I might miss our quarry. That magazine, then another and another and another. My hands ached from the taut grip with which I held each magazine. All the while conscious of the passing of time.

And then a name zoomed up from the page to smack me between the eyes.

"Jacques Manet avec Suzanne Martine."

"Neil!" My voice shockingly loud in the cellar quietness. "Here."

My heart pounding, I inspected the candid shot of the handsome dark-haired man in swimming trunks, stretched across the sand at St. Tropez beside a bikini-clad blonde. What could I tell about Jacques Manet from a photo? I knew by now that he was twenty-six, brilliant, hard-working, hard-playing. *Holly's husband.* What else could a photo tell me? Absurdly, I was annoyed that it couldn't tell me anything.

"That's our lad," Neil confirmed, gazing over my shoulder. "Let's buy the magazine and cut out."

I sat in the car, the magazine across my knees, while Neil swore mildly because traffic, these last few miles, was so unexpectedly heavy.

"I'll get you back in time, Janice," Neil promised, taking advantage of an opening to switch into a faster-moving lane.

"It won't be a disaster if I'm late once," I said defiantly. "I could have driven into Marseille and got hung up in this awful traffic." But my bright red compact sat brazenly on the street in the village. Would someone from the villa drive in and notice?

"I'll leave you at your car and drive back to the garage," Neil decided. "If he's closed, I'll ask around about where he lives. If he identifies Jacques, I'll go straight to Charles Ferney."

"I wish I could call you later," I said wistfully. "I'm dying to know what he says."

"Couldn't you swing a phone call?"

"Not from the villa. I'm there under odd circumstances. If Stephanie knew I was seeing you, she'd flip. She'd figure you were hanging around on the chance of nabbing

Jacques for an interview, using me as a means of keeping tabs on what's happening."

"I could drive out, park near the villa around ten," Neil plotted. "You say the old girl lets you off the hook around then." He frowned. "I'm not sure it's a bright idea for you to wander around at night, after what's happened. No. Forget it, Janice."

"The watchman will be on duty tonight," I rushed to reassure him. I couldn't wait till tomorrow to know that the garage man had confirmed what I was positive was fact—that Jacques was with Holly in that red Ferrari. By ten Neil would have talked with Charles Ferney, too. Perhaps Ferney had come up with something. Suddenly it was urgent to talk to Neil later. "I'll be out for a stroll, Neil. Nothing will happen with the watchman on duty."

"All right—" Neil appeared uneasy. "I'll be no more than a hundred yards down from the gate. I'll be watching for you."

Just before the cut-off that would take us back to the villa, we encountered another traffic snag—cars bumper to bumper, inching along a few feet, stopping, inching along again. For no reason—except that I felt the weight of eyes—I turned to the car beside us. A blue Citroën.

I tensed in shock. Edouard sat behind the wheel, staring coldly at me. Instinctively, my eyes swept to the rear of the car. Helene and Frederic. Neither of them aware of me. Edouard taking Helene on a shopping trip.

Before I could manage a nod of acknowledgement the cars in our lane spurted ahead. The blue Citroën—I recalled now having seen it in the garage—was blocked in immobility.

Edouard had opened the door to Neil when he arrived at the villa to keep his appointment with Jacques. Did Edouard recognize Neil? He must. Would he report this encounter to Stephanie? Had Helene noticed us? I didn't want Stephanie to ease me out of the villa. *I wanted to stay*. Operating again on instinct.

When we pulled up behind my red compact, Neil

reached to draw me close for a moment. His mouth light on mine.

"Relax, Jannie," he coaxed gently. "We're coming in on the home stretch."

I drove to the villa at a greater speed than normal, then jammed the brakes to a screeching stop just before the gate, because a playful St. Bernard pup whose enormous paws foretold his future hugeness romped in blissful ignorance of just-missed death.

"Go on," I scolded. Normally I would have been entranced at his overtures of friendliness. I adore dogs, cats, and children. *"Allez!"*

When he'd finally accepted the message that I would not come out and play, he moved on. I turned in to the villa. The blue Citroën was not in the garage. Edouard must have been delayed in traffic. I was childishly glad not to encounter him just now.

Mme. Simone was standing—small and poignantly alone —before her favorite window in the sitting room, gazing— without seeing, I suspected—at the magnificence of the sunset over the Mediterranean. At the sound of my footsteps she swung about with a welcoming smile.

"Janice, how lovely you look," she said eagerly. I felt guilty that there had been no time to dress for dinner, just a moment to run a brush over my hair, freshen my lipstick, and I'd sprinted downstairs again. "That shade of blue is so becoming."

We settled ourselves on the sofa, waiting for Marie to arrive with the serving wagon. Mme. Simone chattered her usual inanities.

"Oh, we have a night watchman now," she reported coyly. "There was some vandalism at the Rochambeau villa—I'm sure it must have frightened Robert's poor mother half to death. He suggested that Stephanie hire a watch for a few weeks." Stephanie's alibi for the watchman's presence here.

Marie arrived, stolidly served us. Tonight my mind roamed constantly to Neil. My eyes skimmed with traitorous regularity to the exquisite green marble clock that graced the mantel, Neil's words ricocheting through my mind. *"Relax, Jannie. We're coming in on the home stretch."* Coming in winners? Holly's life the prize.

Tonight I was finding it difficult even to appreciate the superb dinner Nicole sent in to us. I knew now that Holly had come within eleven miles of the village. With Jacques. It had to be Jacques.

Charles Ferney spent years with the French Resistance. He must know every corner of this terrain. Holly and Jacques could not have disappeared into the air. They were somewhere within fifteen minutes of the villa. *Let Charles Ferney find Holly.*

"Helene brought me the London *Times* from the city," Mme. Simone corralled me back to the dinner table. "Would you like to read it later? Of course, these days the papers are full of such horrible things." She shuddered in distaste.

The London *Times* wasn't actually her cup of tea, I thought with truant amusement. Mme. Simone preferred the rags that spooned out libelous gossip, personal dirt. Gory murders, way-out torture intrigued her: excitement for a rather desolate existence.

Tonight I waited with more than normal impatience for Mme. Simone to begin to yawn. At ten she was still talking about Robert Rochambeau's villa—modest compared to the Villa Fontaine—where the supposed vandalism presumably took place.

"Robert has been too devoted to his mother all these years to marry. But she's seventy-nine. It's time he thought of himself. He would be good for Stephanie," she said wistfully. "And he's so respected everywhere. They would have his beautiful apartment in Marseille and the villa here." Mme. Simone might be "off" at irregular intervals but she knew the Villa Fontaine was up for sale. She wasn't happy about this.

At a quarter past ten—when I was churning with impatience—Mme. Simone decided it was time to retire.

"Tomorrow Stephanie goes with me into Marseille to my physician," she explained. "To check my new medication. We'll have lunch at the Concorde-Prado." Her pale blue eyes glowed with anticipation.

I hurried from her rooms into the night. I was cold without a jacket in the sea-washed air, but I mustn't waste time when Neil was waiting for me.

"Mademoiselle!" A sharp voice stopped me. "Where do you go?"

"You must be the new watchman." I tried to sound casual. "I'm Janice Carleton. I'm just going out for a stroll along the beach. It's so beautiful." Moonlight spilled upon the driveway.

A flashlight was beamed squarely on my face. I blinked. The beam shot down to hit a page of a notebook in the watchman's hand. He was checking his list of residents at the villa, I guessed.

"Be careful, Mademoiselle," he said sternly. "Do not go far this time of night."

With the scent of summer blossoms lending a poignant beauty to the night I hurried down the driveway, shoulders hunched against the cold. The wrought-iron gates were closed but not locked, because to lock was a travesty when anyone could scale the low stone wall that divided the acreage from the public road.

On the road I turned anxiously to the left, my eyes seeking the black Renault. Car beams blinked on and off not far down. Neil must have seen me in the spill of the moonlight.

He walked forward to meet me. The car was parked at the side in the protective shadows of the lush greenery.

"I was getting nervous," he said quietly. Holding me for a moment.

"What happened, Neil?"

"I showed him the magazine photo," Neil said somberly, "He looked at it a long time. He can't be sure, Janice. The man with Holly wore dark glasses. He simply can't be sure."

CHAPTER ELEVEN

We paused in the shadows. Neil pulled me close, brought his mouth down to mine. Again, for a little while we were two lovers caught up in the miracle of this new discovery of each other. It was as though we had known each other for months rather than days. And then the spell was broken, as it must be in this nightmare.

"I spent an hour with Ferney," Neil reported, striving to lift my spirits. "The man has a fantastically keen mind. He was telling me about the Resistance years, but all the while I knew he was thinking about Jacques. He's not absolutely sure the man with Holly is Jacques," he conceded, "but that won't stop him from going all out to help us. He's working on the assumption that the son of Paul Manet—his Resistance leader—may be in trouble."

"What is he doing?" I persisted. Impatient for the reassurance of details.

"Jannie, we don't ask questions." His eyes gently rebuked me.

"I'm sorry." I was frustrated by my own impotence. But this was the kind of scene in which Charles Ferney was at home. I couldn't have bought this kind of help with money.

"Ferney knows everybody in the area," Neil said. "Every house. If he uncovers the slightest suspicion, he'll know how to operate." In the darkness Neil reached for my hand. "What about lunch tomorrow? Will you be stuck at the villa?"

"No. Stephanie is taking Mme. Simone in to Marseille. They're having lunch there. At the Concorde-Prado," I

117

added. Where they'd been the night Holly and Jacques were supposed to have arrived at the villa. Why couldn't Jacques have called or wired to say they were coming? Then Stephanie would understand this urgency now. Unless, of course, she was responsible for their absence.

"One of these days we'll go into Marseille for dinner," Neil said. "You can't leave without having *bouillabaisse* at the New York."

"The New York?" I laughed, and started because we heard a rustling in the bushes on the other side of the gate. The night watchman, I guessed, curious about my solitary walk.

"Company," Neil whispered, and reached for me. Kissed me lingeringly. So now the watchman would believe this was solely a romantic assignation. He would say nothing at the villa about my being about the grounds at this hour of the night.

"Be careful, Jannie," Neil exhorted. "Lock your door, lock your windows."

He watched me climb up the driveway. Glad, I knew, because the watchman prowled the grounds until daybreak. Even with the watchman there in the shadows, I dreaded the night alone in my room. It would be long before I could wash away the memory of wakening in a dark room with death hovering close by.

Walking up the staircase I heard Stephanie and Celia in the library discussing Celia's favorite Italian couturier. How much of their lives revolved about style! From fragments of an earlier conversation I knew that the men were with Robert at his villa, ironing out segments of the contract. Sadness welled in me for the village people, for Charles Ferney.

In bed I tried to read, hoping this would induce sleep. The windows were locked. I'd tried them twice. The drapes were drawn tight against the night. Logs crackled merrily in the fireplace. I'd decided that again tonight I would leave the bathroom lights on and the door ajar to spill conforting illumination into the bedroom.

Normally I considered it a delicious treat to read in

bed. Tonight I skipped pages. I read without compre-
hending. My mind trod terrifying ground. My anxiety for
Holly was reinforced by the garage man's identification.
Where was she?

I abandoned the book, determinedly shut my eyes, pulled
the light summer blanket about my shoulders. In the
morning Stephanie would phone the Paris office. She
would discover Jacques had not arrived. She would be upset, would throw all her efforts into the search for Holly
and Jacques. Such was my wistful, wishful dream.

I lingered in bed for fully forty minutes after I awoke.
If I were not so disturbed for Holly's welfare, I would
have joyously hopped out of bed, into a swimsuit, down
to that magnificent beach. The water was so blue, seemingly unpolluted at this point. But this morning I lay back
against the pillow, uneasily considering the possibility that
Edouard had alerted Helene to my presence on the autoroute yesterday afternoon. With Neil. Would Edouard
remember Neil?

I fought off unpleasant conjectures. Dress. Go downstairs. I still couldn't gear myself to ring for breakfast in
bed. Stephanie would sleep late as usual. She wouldn't be
calling Paris before ten-thirty. She'd remember, wouldn't
she, about the call?

Yesterday's chill had given way to more normal summer temperature. By noon today would be a scorcher. I
considered a pantsuit, discarded this. I'd be uncomfortably
warm. I reached to pull down the second of my Pucci
copies, designed for traveling and pleasantly flattering to
my slimness.

Dressed and restless, I went downstairs into the morning quietness, still slightly ill-at-at-ease amid such luxury.
The aromatic scent of fresh coffee circulated through the
lower floor. I hovered self-consciously in the foyer, trying
to prod myself into going out to the kitchen to ask for
breakfast.

"Mademoiselle, you did not ring." I whirled about at
the sound of Helene's reproachful voice. She towered

above me, her face an impassive mask. Had Edouard told her yesterday that I was in a car in the next lane? She gave me no inkling. "I will have Marie bring you breakfast on the terrace. It is quite beautiful outside."

"Thank you." I forced a smile.

Helene strode down the corridor in her sensible oxfords, disappeared into the rear of the villa. I walked out onto the terrace, sat down. A faint, warm breeze from the Mediterranean caressed me. For a few moments I gave absorbed attention to a pair of sailboats out on the sea.

My attention roamed. I spied Frederic, about fifty feet from where I sat, spraying a bush of dramatically red roses. He touched a velvet bud here and there with the tenderness I might have bestowed on a beguiling kitten.

Frederic glanced up, startled at my presence. I waved. He paused in indecision, then returned the wave. But a moment later, the spray can under his arm, a pair of roses in hand, he was hurrying towards the side of the villa.

Marie, taciturn as usual, brought me a carafe of coffee. I poured, sipped appreciatively. The coffee was strong, the way I liked it. At irregular intervals my eyes subconsciously moved to my watch, even while I knew Stephanie would not emerge for at least an hour.

I was relieved that she was taking her mother into Marseille. I would have much of the day to spend with Neil. Involuntarily, I shivered. All these days at the villa! So little accomplished.

Marie brought my breakfast tray, graced by a slender vase with two exquisite red roses. Frederic's addition. An American breakfast of scrambled eggs and ham, a platter of fresh-from-the-oven French croissants. I was astonished to discover I was hungry.

I ate with relish, leaned back in my chair to try to relax with a second cup of coffee. I would never truly relax until I saw Holly, could reach out and touch her. Oh, why didn't Stephanie come downstairs early?

I listened tensely for sounds inside the villa. I stiffened when I heard Stephanie—downstairs ahead of schedule —talking to one of the servants.

"Bring me coffee on the terrace," Stephanie ordered with the faintly imperious quality that would have antagonized American domestic help.

"Good morning " I smiled in welcome.

"Good morning, Janice." With an aura of reserve, she sat down at the heavy pine table, directly across from me. "Helene tells me she saw you on the autoroute yesterday."

"Yes." My face was hot. "I drove into Marseille for some sightseeing with a friend." But I'd told her I didn't know anyone here, I recalled quiltily.

"The American who came here searching for Jacques?" she asked with calculated casualness.

"I believe so—" Why was I stammering like a child caught in a lie? I had a right to see Neil.

"Janice, don't let that man use you to dig out information for his magazine article." Her voice was edged with annoyance. "I was furious, the way he tried to force himself into the villa."

"I don't know anything about Jacques," I said realistically. Except that he was married to Holly. And was missing.

"Oh, he is going to try to pump you," Stephanie insisted with impatience. "I know these people."

"We don't discuss the villa," I reassured her quietly. "He's been showing me some of the sights."

Was she sorry she'd invited me to stay here? Was this a polite hint that I should cut out? Alarm brushed me. I didn't want to leave the villa. Not with my inner radar telling me to stay.

"I must drive my mother into Marseille today," Stephanie continued. Unexpectedly her face became cordial. "I'm so pleased that you're here right at this time. Though, of course, I realize the circumstances are not happy," she sympathized. "But Maman is delighted to have you, and I'm free to devote myself to Celia."

Marie brought fresh coffee for Stephanie. While Stephanie sipped appreciatively, I tried to gear myself to tell her that Holly and Jacques had been seen at a garage only eleven miles from the villa. Yet how could I, when the garage man had been unable to make a positive identification of Jacques? And what good would it do to remind her to call Paris, since she didn't believe Jacques was married?

I could tell her what Neil's contact in Rome had reported. That Jacques had been seen in Rome ten days ago, in the company of a beautiful blonde American. But Rome was full of blonde Americans in the summer. Oh, let Neil's Rome contact come up with a copy of the marriage license!

Awkwardly, I excused myself, left Stephanie, went out to the garage for my rented car. I drove into the village, searingly hot in the late-morning sun. Relief welled in me when I saw Neil sitting at our usual table on the café terrace.

I parked, left the car, rapidly crossed the traffic-free street to his table, aware of the contemptuous curiosity of a pair at a nearby table. They loathed the tourist invasion—particularly tourists who were part of the villa scene, who·threatened the whole existence of their town as they had always known it.

"Hi." Neil's smile was warm and cheerful. But it was belied by the seriousness of his eyes. Like me he was painfully aware of the passage of time—and our lack of progress.

"Have you had any word from Rome?" I asked breathlessly, sliding into a chair across from him.

"Nothing yet." Neil frowned, glanced sideways at the pair at the next table. "They're listening in," he said quietly. "They were carrying on bitterly before about the presence of Stephanie's houseguests. Feelings are ugly, Janice. They're particularly bitter that Jacques isn't here to stop the sale."

"They're so quick to condemn!" I flared.

"To them it looks bad," Neil pointed out gently. "They don't realize Jacques is missing."

"Neil—" My mind was diverging onto a dozen tracks. "Suppose I flew to Rome? Tried to contact some of Holly's friends from that movie crowd?"

"What would that accomplish?"

"If Holly had been dating Jacques, they might know. They might even know that Holly and Jacques are married. Neil—" I leaned forward urgently. "Perhaps they know *where* Holly and Jacques were married."

"What about a phone call instead?" Neil suggested, more practical than I. "I assume you have names we can try?"

"A couple." Eagerly, I dug into my purse. I had with me the last two letters from Holly. "I know where she was staying."

I brought out the letters, handed one to Neil. We read them carefully, searching for leads. Holly mentioned several people in the company. By first names.

"What about the producer?" Neil probed. "The director?"

"The director is a man named Jock Townsend," I recalled. "An American. I don't know where he was staying."

"We'll try Holly's hotel first," Neil said briskly. "I know half a dozen other places where he might be staying—if he's still in Rome. Probably, there was work to do to wrap up the film. That would have kept him there for a while. Have some coffee, and we'll drive over to Ferney's place and phone from there."

Ferney greeted us with quiet cordiality, listened to my report of the morning's encounter with Stephanie.

"Stephanie would prefer to believe that nothing is wrong." he said dryly. "Her personal plans might be upset. But we are looking for Jacques and your sister, Janice," he reassured me quietly. "These things take time." How could I be sure that time was not running out for Holly?

Neil briefed Ferney on our need to use his phone.

"Use it," Ferney agreed readily. "Few calls come for me."

"Let's try Holly's hotel first," Neil decided. "Then the others."

I sat restlessly on a folding chair beside the desk while Neil sought to reach Jock Townsend. Ferney was outside at the gas pump, carrying on a leisurely conversation with a truckdriver who'd pulled in for gas. Was Ferney truly trying to help us—or was this a cloak-and-dagger reproduction of his Resistance days? Instantly I felt guilty that I could think so cynically.

Forty minutes later, Neil relinquished the phone with disgust. I added up the toll calls we'd made, pulled out franc notes to reimburse Charles Ferney. Less expensive than a flight to Rome, I conceded.

"Any luck?" Ferney strolled into the tiny office.

"We came up with nothing," Neil sighed. "Maybe with inflation hitting Rome so badly Americans are all retreating to the less expensive *pensions*. But I'll have my Rome contact try to check this out."

Ferney glanced at the small clock on his desk.

"It is time for the midday meal. Come with me to my house. We will eat together and talk."

Ferney closed up for the traditional European long luncheon. The three of us crossed the road, walked along the white sand beach to his small cottage. The shutters were closed against the heat of the sun. Ferney opened the door, swung it wide so that we might enter.

There was one huge room with a kitchen alcove; it was unexpectedly cool in contrast to the outdoor heat. Ferney crossed to open the shutters that faced the sea, allowing a pleasant breeze to enter.

I glanced about the modestly but comfortably furnished room. The walls were stuccoed; the fireplace was faced with aged bricks. Rough-hewn bookcases—stained oak—lined one wall. Above the fireplace was a gun display. I knew these must be relics of his Resistance days, kept here as Paul Manet had maintained his room of mementos at the villa, to keep forever fresh the memory of France's dark years.

"Sit at the table," Ferney urged, pointing to the heavy pine table flanked by four captain's chairs. "We will soon eat."

Curiously, I read the titles of a few of Ferney's books. His tastes were eclectic. He was a well-read man. Across the room Neil was inspecting a group of photographs. Ferney's children, I guessed, who had moved away because the fishing village offered so little for the young.

"If the garage man had not been new in town," Ferney remarked as he walked back into the room with a tray laden with bread, cheeses, a plate of paté, and fruit, "he would surely have recognized Jacques. The man who owned it before was growing old—he sold it to go and live at his brother's vineyard."

"He recognized Holly," I reminded. "He said they were in a red Ferrari."

Ferney straightened up. His eyes focused sharply on me.

"Jacques' father always drove a Ferrari. Always red."

"So Jacques was being sentimental," I said shakily, "when he gave Holly a red Ferrari for a wedding present." Now no doubts lingered in Charles Ferney's mind. He was sure the man with Holly was Jacques.

"It is the sort of thing I would expect of Jacques, yes." Ferney was bringing down wineglasses, a bottle of wine from a cabinet against the wall. "Jacques was very close to his father. He was very young, remember, when his mother died. Sometimes Paul would bring the boy with him over to my house, and Jacques would sit there—his eyes so big and solemn—while we talked about the old days. Jacques loved the village. It was a magnificent treat for him to be allowed to go out in one of the fishing vessels. That is why it is such a shock to see that Jacques is permitting Stephanie to go ahead with the sale of the villa. If he were insistent, Rochambeau would not allow this. This is what happened when the English syndicate tried earlier to buy the villa."

"Jacques is in no position to stop him," I reminded unhappily. "Don't blame Jacques."

"It could be that Jacques needs the money to finance the new plant you've hoped for in the village," Neil pointed out cautiously. "This new fabric he has developed is revolutionary. A plant here to manufacture it could

transform the village into a thriving industrial commu-
nity."

"That we could accept, with gratitude," Ferney said
sternly, sitting with us at the table. "But not the monstros-
ity of a resort and a gambling casino. How can Jacques
let this happen to us? And it will go through. There is a
young woman in the small office Rochambeau maintains
in town. She tells us it is a matter of, perhaps, two or
three days. The sale will go through. The village will die."

"But Jacques can stop the sale—you say that Rochambeau would not vote against him if he were insistent. Find
Jacques!"

"What about Rochambeau?" Neil asked keenly. "What
kind of a man is he?"

"I do not like him," Ferney said emphatically.

"Why?" Signals were clanging in my head.

"Rochambeau lives among us, but he is aloof, considering himself above the villagers. He remains in his villa
only to appease his mother. And then, of course, there is
Stephanie."

"How long has that been going on?" Neil leaned forward intently while we helped ourselves from the tray of
food.

"I think Rochambeau has been in love with Stephanie—in his cautious fashion—since Paul brought her
home twelve years ago," Ferney said. "But only in this
last year have they been seeing so much of each other.
Stephanie grows older—she is spending more time at the
villa. I gather she has indicated an interest in Rochambeau. At the same time, I suspect, he is uneasy about her
extravagances, her way of life. He lives well, but not in
the manner of Stephanie Manet."

"If the villa is sold, Stephanie will be a very rich
woman," Neil guessed. "I should think Rochambeau
wants the sale to go through."

"You are searching for a motive, my friend." Ferney
smiled indulgently. "If we knew who wanted Jacques and
Holly out of the way, we would be halfway to discovering
them." But they hadn't been in the closed-off wing of the

villa, my mind pinpointed. Could Robert Rochambeau be responsible for their disappearance?

"It could be Rochambeau." I leaned forward earnestly. "M. Ferney, could they be somewhere in his villa?"

"That is a wild guess," he edged. But he was thoughtful. "Rochambeau is pressed for money. His villa, though smaller than the Villa Fontaine, is expensive to maintain. And he has an apartment in Marseille. Yes, we must check on Robert," Ferney agreed. "While he lives in an aura of deep respectability, there have been deals which I have questioned. Legal, yes—but ethically not what one would expect of Rochambeau. The sale of the villa—making Stephanie a very rich woman—could be most important to him."

"What about the Resistance years?" Neil asked curiously. "Was he living here in the village?"

"Robert Rochambeau," Ferney reported dryly, "was inactive during the Resistance. His mother even then was an invalid." An ironic smile touched his mouth. "Rochambeau's sole contribution to the Resistance was to practice regularly at a shooting range so that he might protect his mother against possible physical harm. Even now Rochambeau takes pride in his skill in shooting, though it never goes beyond the shooting range. He does not even hunt."

"Could he be holding Holly and Jacques at his villa until the sale goes through?" Neil probed.

"How could he explain the kidnapping later?" I demanded.

"There are men for hire, Janice," Ferney said gently. "If Rochambeau wanted to do this, he would know how to handle it."

"There's another angle," Neil brought up. "Could it be that some villager believes that, as long as Jacques is unable to appear, the sale can't go through?"

"But everything is going ahead, Neil! Nobody's waiting for Jacques to appear."

"Wait, Janice—let us consider this," Ferney exhorted.

"There may be those in the village who believe Jacques must be present at the signing of the contracts."

"So they're holding Jacques and Holly to prevent the sale!" I pounced.

"Possibly," Ferney conceded. "Still, I cannot believe that anyone in the village would try to kill you, Janice."

"A psychotic would," Neil pointed out quietly. "And feelings run dangerously high in the village about the prospective resort."

Ferney squinted in thought.

"During the Resistance years there were times when the hackles at the back of my neck have warned me of approaching danger—or have alerted me when we were approaching something big. I have that feeling now. Neil, that map you have," he said briskly. "Bring it out. Let us inspect it closely. Somewhere within a very small circumference Jacques and Holly are being held prisoners. Every inch of that area must be covered. Within the next twenty-four hours!"

CHAPTER TWELVE

"I must return to reopen the station," Ferney said finally with an apologetic smile. "Walk along the beach for a while. Relax," he coaxed Neil and me. "You two have done all that you can. I have a dozen men searching today. The Resistance may be thirty years behind us, but we have not forgotten how to operate."

"I'm so grateful," I said earnestly. "But there must be places we can look."

"Not as well as my men," Ferney refuted gently. "They are away from their jobs today. Because Paul Manet's son is in trouble. They can go where Neil and you may not." He rose resolutely to his feet, his eyes focused on the clock. "If there is word, I will receive a call. Check with me from time to time. If I have closed the station, call here—" He reached for a scrap of paper, scribbled down the number.

Ferney walked away from the beach cottage in the direction of his station. Neil and I headed in the opposite direction, my hand in his. Somber at first. Then, with a chuckle, Neil paused to kick off his loafers.

"Get rid of your shoes," he ordered. "Let's walk in the sand. It feels great."

We walked barefoot in comfortable silence for a while. Neil's hand withdrew from mine. His arm moved about my waist. I lifted my face to his. His lips brushed mine.

"Relax, Jannie," he coaxed. "We're coming in on the home stretch." He'd told me that before. With the same conviction.

These would have been incredibly precious minutes if I

were not distraught about Holly. Back in New York Neil and I might have passed each other on the street. We had to jet across the Atlantic to meet. That would please Holly's sense of drama.

"Let's wade," Neil suggested, taking my shoes from my hand to drop them into a heap with his own.

"Like this?" I protested, but Neil was already pulling me towards the sea. "Neil!" I laughingly objected, but he was drawing me into the gentle surf.

Hand in hand we walked along the water's edge, enchanted with the deliciousness of the water, the caressing warmth of the sun. After a while we deserted the water to stretch on the white sand, talked about the glory of southern France. Yet all the while I hovered on the edge of a mental precipice, feeling myself closer and closer to Holly—yet terrified of what the moment of discovery might reveal.

Sun-kissed, with the taste of the sea in our mouths, we walked back to the gas station to talk again with Ferney.

"No. No reports yet from any of the men," he said quietly. "But we will hear. They will be out through the day and into the night," he promised. "Every inch of ground will be covered. If there is news, Janice, I will phone you at the villa." Unexpectedly Ferney grinned. "For something like that I will bring myself to call the villa."

Neil and I drove back into the village. The café terrace was shaded at this time of the afternoon. Feeling oddly at loose ends, we decided to sit at a table, order ice cream. Neil spied a copy of the international *Herald Tribune* at the next table, leaned over to appropriate it as the waiter approached us.

"A record number of college kids in Europe this summer," Neil reported. "I'll bet plenty of them are disillusioned."

The waiter hovered above us, less disapproving than I remembered. We were beginning to be accepted. Still, I recalled, Neil made a point of inspecting the checks here before he paid. They were not above padding. They couldn't pad much when we were just ordering ice cream, I thought humorously.

The waiter withdrew. I tried to concentrate on the section of newspaper Neil had handed over to me. I was conscious of a painful restlessness. My inner radar sent up distress signals.

Neil was startled when I said I thought I ought to drive back to the villa.

"It's early," he protested, reaching for my hand.

"I'm beat," I confessed. "I've been sleeping so badly. I might conk out for an hour before dinner." In daylight I might be able to sleep.

"Good idea," he approved, squeezing my hand reassuringly. "I'll walk you to your car."

I drove back to the villa with a disquieting sense of urgency. Pulling into the garage I saw Edouard at one side, absorbed in cleaning a rifle. He glanced up at my approach, his face hard, angry. I turned cold at the active hate in his eyes. Then he lowered his eyes to the rifle again, as though he hadn't seen me.

The grey Rolls and the white Citroën were missing. The Whitneys and David Carey were away from the villa, I surmised. Stephanie had driven her mother into Marseille and had not yet returned. I left the garage, headed for the villa.

Somewhere at the side—I could hear their voices but I couldn't see them—Helene was scolding Frederic. While she loved him with a poignant intensity, she held him on a tight rein. Probably, I thought with compassion, because she was anxious for his wellbeing. I knew that Edouard and Marie took a spiteful pleasure in teasing him.

I went upstairs to my room, kicked off my shoes, replaced my Pucci copy with a tricot mini-robe, stretched across the bed. I locked the door, even though the sun still streamed into the room. Because I was so tired—for the moment not fearful of an intruder—I fell asleep.

An hour later I awoke with a jarring start. A car was pulling up the driveway. I arose from the bed, crossed to a window. The white Citroën. Stephanie and Mme. Simone were returning from Marseille.

I went into the luxurious bathroom, ran hot water into the magnificent marble tub, chose a dress for dinner. The evening would drag endlessly. I would have to sit across the table and listen attentively to Mme. Simone, while every minute I would wonder about the progress of the dozen men Charles Ferney had combing the area. Every time the phone rang I would almost stop breathing because it might be Ferney calling me.

The short, sharp knock at the door startled me. I hurried to answer. With my hand on the knob I instinctively hesitated.

"Who is it?"

"Helene, Mademoiselle."

I opened the door, glad that my robe gave me an excuse for this hesitancy at opening.

"Yes, Helene?" Was Mme. Simone letting me off the hook for dinner tonight? Perhaps she was tired from the trip into Marseille.

"Mme. Simone would like to have dinner at seven tonight if that would not inconvenience you," Helene said in her deep, almost mannish tones.

"That'll be fine." I forced myself to smile. "I'll be down at seven."

"And Madame Manet wishes me to tell you," Helene continued. "There was a call this afternoon from M. Jacques. He has been tied up on business. He will arrive at the villa late Monday."

"Thank you." Trembling, I struggled to mask my shock. "Thank you, Helene."

I shut the door. Stood there, Helene's words echoing in my brain. Jacques would be here late Monday. He had called. What did Helene say? I tried impatiently to reconstruct her exact words. *"There was a call this afternoon from M. Jacques. He will arrive late Monday."*

Not *they* will arrive, my mind pinpointed. *"He has been tied up on business."* Exactly what Stephanie has said. If Jacques Manet was not with Holly, who was the man with her at the garage? In the red Ferrari. All along I had been so positive that Jacques and Holly were together. Suddenly everything was upside down.

Mechanically I went into the bathroom, let the water run out of the tub. What about Charles Ferney? Would he abandon the search if he knew Holly's companion was someone other than Jacques Manet?

But how could this man have fooled Holly? No! She's too bright. I won't believe that Jacques isn't with her! Someone wants me to believe Jacques called this afternoon. That he isn't with Holly. This is a ruse to get me to call off the search!

Who could have received the call about Jacques? Not Stephanie—she was in Marseille with Mme. Simone. One of the servants must have taken the call. Edouard? Usually he answered the phone when he was working indoors.

My hands were trembling as I struggled to zip the closing at the back of my dress. Should I try to phone Neil? No, I mustn't take that chance. I know how Stephanie feels about him. I want to remain here at the villa at least until Monday evening—when Jacques is supposed to show. I mustn't give Stephanie any cause to ask me to leave the villa.

I ran a brush over my hair, touched a lipstick to my mouth, turning over in my mind the possibility that Edouard was involved in this telephone call that was supposed to have come from Jacques. I frowned impatiently at the deep circles beneath my eyes, advertising my lack of sleep these past few nights.

All right, I ordered myself impatiently. Go downstairs. Gear yourself for dinner with Mme. Simone. I wished, painfully, that I dared to phone Neil right now.

I arrived downstairs simultaneously with the serving cart. Marie was her usual sullen self. Mme. Simone welcomed me with a flutter of pleasure, though she appeared rather tired. I suspected this would be an early evening.

When Mme. Simone released me, I'd drive into town, phone Neil. Would he be at his *pension?* I'd take a chance. If not there, perhaps he'd be at Ferney's house. I could phone from the café.

I sat down at the table, preparing myself to push through the next two hours of small talk. All the while Helene's message about Jacques's purported phone call chiseled away at my nerves. If the call was not a hoax, then who was with Holly?

"It was such a delight to be in Marseille," Mme. Simone bubbled while Marie ladled carrot soup into white porcelain dishes. "I adore the city. And the doctor was so pleased with my reaction to this new medication."

I tried to appear interested as Mme. Simone prattled about their sumptuous luncheon at the Concorde-Prado, about the afternoon shopping. Coyly she produced a tiny, charming purse mirror she had bought for me.

"It's lovely," I said, touched that she had made this gesture. "Thank you."

Marie appeared to clear away the soup plates, to serve us crisp duckling—a favorite of Mme. Simone's. Tiny roast potatoes, green beans, and a salad accompanied the duck. A gourmet meal—but I was hardly in the mood to appreciate Nicole's efforts.

By the time Marie arrived with our *baba au rhum* and coffee, my smile was strained. It was early. I feared Mme. Simone would dawdle forever over dessert.

Surprisingly, over our second cups of coffee, Mme. Simone began to yawn, despite the early hour.

"You've had a long day," I sympathized. Hopefully.

"All that running about does tire me," she conceded wistfully. "Perhaps I'll turn in early tonight." The faded blue eyes rested curiously on me. "Janice, what do you do for amusement in the evenings? It must be so dull for you."

"I read," I said quickly.

"Have you talked to Charles Ferney about your sister?"

"Not yet," I fabricated. Startled. I'd forgotten that Mme. Simone had recommended this. "I'll talk with him tomorrow." Perhaps I'd talk to him tonight.

"He'll find your sister for you," she prophesied, and my

heart thumped. "I have an instinct about such things. And then you'll leave the villa. I'll miss you, Janice."

Ten minutes later I was up in my room collecting a light coat against the night chill. Running downstairs again I could hear the animated conversation in the formal dining room.

"Of course I was upset when that man threw the tomato at the car as we drove through the village," Celia was saying virtuously. "But then I remembered the mentality of these people and I understood."

I cut through the side, en route to the garage. A fog was settling about the grounds. I hoped it wouldn't grow heavier. I hated driving in fog.

The night watchman would say nothing about my driving out tonight. Why should he? He was there to keep out intruders. He'd assume I was out for a romantic assignation. Nothing to report to the villa.

I slid behind the wheel of the car, tried to recall what I'd been told about the lights. This was my first experience at driving the rented car at night. There. The headlights thrust broad circlets of illumination on the garage wall. The lights were all right.

I backed out slowly. A window squeaked open above the garage. Involuntarily I glanced upward. Edouard was at the window, checking on who was going out. All right, I thought defensively, let him tell Stephanie I drove away in the evening. I wasn't a prisoner at the villa. I was entitled to a social life.

Then I stared sharply at the brilliantly lighted upstairs window. Edouard was not alone. A woman had moved into view. Celeste. Edouard's arm shot upward. He jerked the shade down to the sill.

I moved slowly down the road, braked to a standstill as a flashlight focused on the windshield. The night watchman. He crossed to the car, squinted inside, smiled broadly.

"Drive carefully, Mademoiselle," he urged. "The fog is coming in heavy."

He strode towards the gates to swing them wide for me.

I drove through, waved a jaunty farewell. My hands were tense on the wheel as I leaned forward for a clearer view of the fog-shrouded road ahead. Visibility was discomfortingly limited.

The drive into the village consumed triple the normal time because of the fog. Each turn appeared different. Twice I was fearful that I'd swung right too soon. And then—through the thick fog—I saw the village rising before me in its night garb. A cluster of cars was parked before the café. Across the narrow street a raucous record played at top volume in a flat above the bakery. A few doors down, half a dozen teenagers hovered about a hotrod.

I parked, walked self-consciously into the café, a stranger to me at this hour. The lights were very low—candles in netted jars on each table. I spied a waiter I knew, hurried to ask if I might use the telephone. I knew the only pay telephone in the village was in the shop long closed up for the night.

"This way, Mademoiselle." His eyes knowing as they dwelt on me.

"Thank you." I slipped two francs into his hand.

I fished out the phone number of Neil's *pension*, dialed. The phone rang repeatedly before his landlady picked it up, her tone saying she was annoyed at this interruption.

"I do not believe M. Grant is in his room," she informed me stiffly.

"I would be so grateful if you would try him," I cajoled.

"One minute, Mademoiselle," she agreed impatiently.

I heard her calling sharply up the stairs. Perhaps she was right, I thought with misgivings. Why should Neil sit around in a grubby room? He was barely seventeen miles from Marseille, a swinging city in the evening.

"Neil Grant *ici*," he said brightly.

"Neil, I'm at the café," I said breathlessly. So glad that he was home. "Could you drive over?"

"I'll be there in fifteen minutes. Jannie, are you all right?" Concern coating his voice.

"I'm fine," I reassured him. "I just want to talk with you. Oh, drive carefully. The fog's awful."

"Give me an extra five minutes," he compromised.

I went to a corner table, ordered a liqueur and coffee, conscious of the curious glances beamed in my direction. An aggressive Frenchman—reeking of cheap wine—swaggered over to make a mild pitch.

"I am waiting for a friend," I said coldly.

He shrugged, returned to his own table, interest evaporated. The waiter brought my liqueur and coffee. I sipped at the pungent sweetness of the liqueur, my eyes on the shadowed entrance to the café, even though I knew it would be a while before Neil would appear. What would Neil's reaction be when I told him Jacques was supposed to have phoned the villa this afternoon? Instinct told me it had not been Jacques. Would reason tell Neil the same?

Across the room—smoke-filled and wine-scented—a trio of Frenchmen were talking with loud contempt about the sprinkling of tourists who passed through the village. The Americans were especially disliked.

"Wait," one of them warned. "Wait till the English buy the villa. You will find Americans climbing through your windows."

The conversation grew bawdy. A waiter tried to quiet them. I concentrated on my coffee. Another waiter joined the first. The trio was good-humoredly escorted to the door, despite their noisy indignation.

I stared somberly as the door closed behind them. It would be a long time before I could accept this French hostility towards Americans. And then the door was almost immediately opened to admit a new patron. Not until he was well into the room did I recognize him. *Edouard.*

I lifted my coffee cup to my mouth, seemingly preoccupied. He walked to a table no more than ten feet from mine, sat down with a bearded Frenchman whom he apparently knew. But it was a casual meeting—unplanned. In the heavily shadowed room our eyes met for one stinging instant. Then he withdrew his glance. Beckoned to the waiter, ignoring my presence.

My initial instinct was to flee. Edouard had followed me here. *Why?* I couldn't leave. Neil would arrive at any moment. I didn't dare leave. Edouard might follow me out into the night street. Why was he here? What kind of threat did I present to him?

My hand was unsteady as I brought the coffee cup up to my mouth again. My mind was agonizingly active. Had Edouard kidnapped Holly and Jacques? Had they arrived at the villa and been spirited away by Edouard, acting on someone else's orders? Edouard was not of the village. Mme. Simone had said he'd been hired in Marseille. Hired by whom?

When Neil arrived we must go to Charles Ferney, tell him about Edouard. Ferney would know what to do. Again, I had a sense of hovering on the brink of discovery, feeling Holly so dramatically close to me. Where was she? Where?

I kept my eyes on the door. Disappointed, twice, when the new arrival was not Neil. Then the door opened again and Neil walked in. His eyes swept the room until they lit on me. I lifted a hand in welcome.

Neil swiftly crossed to join me at my corner table.

"You were right," he said casually. "The fog is rotten. I was practically hanging out the car window, trying to see the side of the road."

"Neil, Edouard is here," I whispered. "At the second table to the left. He came in right after I did."

"Did he know you were going out tonight?" Neil managed a cautious squint in Edouard's direction.

"Yes. He was at the window above when I pulled out of the garage. Celeste was there with him." I struggled to sound matter-of-fact. "There's more, Neil," I said quickly because he was about to speak. "There was a phone call at the villa. Presumably from Jacques. Stephanie was away. One of the servants answered—"

"Who?"

"I don't know. I was afraid to ask. Stephanie sent Helene up to tell me. Jacques said—*if* it was Jacques—that he'd been tied up on business and would arrive at the villa late Monday."

My eyes clung to Neil's face as he pondered this unexpected development.

"We don't know if it was Jacques," he said slowly, confirming my suspicion. "On the other hand, it could have been Jacques and Holly could be with him—and all this could be a ghastly nightmare."

"Then how would you account for the rock through my window?" I challenged. "The man in my room? Neil, that couldn't have been Jacques."

"Someone is stalling for time," Neil decided. "Needing until Monday night—" Then he was silent because the waiter was at our table.

Neil ordered wine for both of us. Conscious of Edouard's presence two tables away, we kept our voices muted as we dissected this new situation, tried to fit it into the framework of what we knew.

"We'll drive out to Ferney's cottage," Neil said when we'd made a pretense of drinking our wine. "He may have some constructive ideas about this."

"It isn't too late?"

"Ferney runs a gas station because this makes him his own boss," Neil said humorously. "And it allows him long evenings for reading. Besides, he isn't apt to be sleeping when he's involved in this kind of operation."

We left the café, headed for the Renault. Neil shot backward glances over his shoulder to be sure we were not followed. Close by on the water, a foghorn blared. Spine-chilling. Neil reached for my hand, squeezed it reassuringly for a moment before we seated ourselves in the car.

We inched along the road, at last seeing the fog-hazed lights in Ferney's cottage. We parked, walked down the beach to his door, knocked lightly.

"Who is it?" His voice was a controlled monotone.

"Neil and Janice."

Swiftly he opened the door. We walked inside. While

Ferney closed the door, carefully bolted it, Neil and I inspected the huge chart taped to one stuccoed wall. Every road in the area was obviously drawn in. Houses indicated. Sections marked off in red pencil. Others shaded in with ink. On the table before the chart a walkie-talkie was set up for operation. All the tools of the underground.

"That's our territory," Ferney said. "Areas shaded with ink have been checked out. By tomorrow night every inch within a twelve-mile radius will have been searched. I myself do not move fast enough these years—particularly on damp nights—to be of much use out there," he apologized. "I must be content to direct operations from here." His eyes swept from Neil to me with sudden awareness. "You have some news."

Neil briefed him on the phone call, on Edouard's appearance at the café.

"We must check on Edouard," he said vigorously. "Who hired him?"

"I don't know—" Regretfully I shook my head. "I don't even know his last name."

"We will find out." Ferney reached for the phone.

Neil stationed himself before the chart, squinting at the penciled notations while Ferney talked on the phone. The first four calls netted him nothing. Grimly he rang again.

"Odette," he said quietly when someone responded at the other end. "I need some information. There is a man working at the Villa Fontaine. Edouard. Would you know anything about him?" He listened, frowning. "Odette, you know you can trust me," he interjected with a touch of irritation. "What do you know?" Neil deserted the chart to stand beside Ferney. Ferney was listening attentively to the woman at the other end. "Thank you, Odette," he said with gratitude a few moments later. "Yes, it is most helpful." He put down the phone, turned to Neil and me. "Odette manages Rochambeau's small local office. She tells me that Rochambeau hired Edouard on Stephanie's behalf. Edouard had just evaded a long jail sentence through Rochambeau's legal maneuverings."

"Edouard was put into the villa so that Rochambeau

could know exactly what was happening there," Neil guessed.

"Edouard owes his freedom to Rochambeau. He must do what Rochambeau demands." I took a deep breath. "Even if that includes murder."

"You think the man in your room was Edouard?" Ferney asked.

"You said the man was six feet tall," Neil reminded. "Edouard must be five inches shorter."

"I could have been wrong," I said uneasily. "I was so frightened I could have thought him six feet tall."

"Janice, you mustn't go back to the villa tonight," Neil began.

"I must!" I interrupted. "If I don't show, he would know we suspect him. They might—they might do something desperate."

"She's right," Ferney seconded this. "Now we know we must concentrate on Rochambeau—but he mustn't be aware of this. Tonight she must go back to the villa, Neil."

The phone jangled, harsh in the tension-laden room. Ferney reached to pick it up. His voice was cool, businesslike, belying the inner pressures.

"For you, Neil—" He held the phone outstretched.

"I took the liberty of giving your number to my Rome contact," Neil explained, reaching for the phone. I leaned forward, my heart pounding. "Hello—" Neil listened, bird-dog alert. "Right. I've got it. Thanks, Craig. I'll keep in touch." Neil put down the phone, turned to me. "Jacques Manet and Holly Carleton were married two weeks ago at Frascati, south of Rome. We'll have a photostat of the marriage license by the next mail."

CHAPTER THIRTEEN

"Stephanie will be astonished," Ferney said dryly. "She was positive no one would ever catch Jacques."

"It isn't so vital to have the photostat now," Neil pointed out with a diffident smile. "Nobody could match your search for Jacques and Holly."

"If they are being held within this area," Ferney promised, "we will most certainly know by tomorrow night. And we will move in."

I contemplated a possible explosive scene with Stephanie with distaste.

"I won't tell Stephanie about the marriage certificate," I decided. "We don't need the Manets now." With Ferney's old Resistance group in operation, we were in the best possible hands. Holly would relish the drama of this, later.

"There is a meeting at the villa tomorrow evening," Ferney reported. His source of information was probably the woman in Rochambeau's local office, Odette. "The village officials are to have dinner with the English buyers."

"Can't they stop the building of the resort complex?" I asked. "I mean—through some speedily passed zoning regulation?" I couldn't envision the village officials dining with the so-hated purchasers of the villa.

"The Villa Fontaine is beyond the village jurisdiction," Ferney explained wryly. "What the English are doing, actually, is to make a conciliatory move towards the villagers in the hope of avoiding unpleasant incidents later. They are well aware of the mood in the village. This consultation of our elected officials," he wound up cynically, "comes under the heading of diplomacy."

"I don't like Janice's going back to the villa tonight," Neil said stubbornly to Ferney. "How do we know what Edouard might try?" Provided he was working for Rochambeau. Provided Rochambeau wished me silenced.

"Neil, we just went through this," I said hastily. "I must go back. Pretend as though we know nothing. We can't gamble with Holly's and Jacques's lives."

"Edouard did not follow you?" Ferney questioned sharply.

"I'm sure he didn't," Neil said. "He would have had to be right on our tail in this fog. No, he couldn't have followed us."

"There is a watchman on the grounds, is there not?" Ferney turned solicitously towards me.

"Yes."

"Ask him to accompany you up to the house," Ferney ordered. "I will go down the road to a friend's house. He will loan me a pair of walkie-talkies. Neil will follow you to the villa, remain in his car close by. When you are inside your room, call him on the walkie-talkie."

"Yes." Neil nodded vigorously, his smile to me encouraging.

"Stay there, Neil, until you see Edouard return. If you drive slowly past the villa, you will see if he returns to his own quarters above the garage."

"In this fog?" I questioned.

"The lights from the servants' quarters will be visible from the road. Try this, anyway," he urged. "Wait a while, Neil. Make sure Janice is all right. Then come back here. You can sleep on the couch there."

"I'm not concerned about sleeping tonight," Neil brushed this aside.

"We can spell each other," Ferney said. "It will be a long night."

Neil and I sat on the worn, black-leather sofa, hearing the faint sounds of the sea, while Ferney drove down the road to his friend's house to borrow the walkie-talkies.

"Relax, Jannie," Neil coaxed, an arm about my shoulders. "Ferney's crew will find Holly and Jacques. It's going to be okay."

"Oh, Neil, I hope so!"

His arms closed in about me. His mouth reached for mine. I felt so safe with Neil. For a fragment of time anxiety was forgotten. It was as though I'd waited all my life to meet him—impossible to believe we'd known each other only a few days.

In less than ten minutes Ferney was back inside the cottage, having obtained the necessary pair of walkie-talkies.

"Armand's wife likes to keep tabs on him when he is out in the boat fishing," Ferney explained with a chuckle.

I listened attentively while Ferney briefed us on the operation of the walkie-talkies.

"At this hour of the night it is not likely anyone else will be operating on this frequency," Ferney guessed, "but nevertheless, be general in what you say. 'The weather is fine' if all is well. If you anticipate trouble, 'a storm is coming up.' In which case Neil will alert me via walkie-talkie and I will join him. I know the villa well—if you are in trouble, we will come." Ferney stared searchingly at Neil. "Do you wish to be armed?"

"I think I should be," Neil acknowledged casually. Suddenly, my heart was pounding.

"Take this one." Ferney reached above the fireplace for a revolver. "I'll give you bullets."

Ferney walked with Neil and me to the Renault, sitting in a fog that was about the worst I'd ever encountered.

"Don't use the revolver unless you must," Ferney exhorted.

Neil grinned faintly.

"I promise you I won't." He reached to open the car door. "I'll wait half an hour after I see the lights go dark above the garage, if I can see them. If I can't, Jannie, I'll get the message across to you—you'll have to clue me in. Half an hour after the windows go dark," he reiterated, "I'll cut out. I'll come back here."

"Will the walkie-talkie pick up from the villa to here?" I asked. "All those miles?"

"That depends on the weather," Ferney conceded. "But Neil and you will have no trouble communicating. Possibly you will be able to contact me here," he offered somberly. He'd said he'd come if I were in trouble. How could he know if the walkie-talkies were ineffective?

Neil and I drove in silence, my head pillowed on Neil's shoulder. Fog rolled in ominously around us, impeding our progress. Holly and Jacques were married. The words flashed—ticker-tape fashion—across my mind. No doubts now. Not that *I* had doubted. And in this awful fog a dozen men crept through the night searching for them.

The village was asleep except for the café, where a male chorus sang raucously. Neil walked me to the red compact, the windshield and the windows opaque with steam.

"I'll drive ahead so you can follow my lights," he decided. "Don't worry about tailgating. I want you close. I won't go over fifteen kilometers in this soup."

I leaned over the wheel, watching for the red of Neil's rear lights. There! He was moving. I lifted my foot from the brake, shifted it to the gas pedal, my gaze fastened to the red circlets at either end of Neil's bumper, feeling safe when he was only a few feet ahead, guiding me.

We traveled slowly, passing no one on the way. Then Neil was pulling off the road. A hand beckoned me to continue on. I pulled up beside him, lowered the window on his side.

"The villa's just ahead." His voice low, though it was hardly likely we would be overheard. "When you come to the gate, honk. The watchman will open it for you. He knows you're out."

"Suppose somebody hears up at the house?" I hedged.

"On a night like this, people lean on their horns," Neil said. "Don't worry about what they think." He reached for my hand. "Drive over to Ferney's when you're free in the morning. I'll be going to my place to pick up the mail, but I'll come right back."

"Neil—" I tried to sound calm. "If anything comes through tonight, will you call me on the walkie-talkie?"

"No," he rejected gently. "I won't have you lying awake all night. And you will if you expect me to call."

At the gate I touched the horn lightly, my foot on the brake. I was conscious of the walkie-talkie concealed in the pocket of my rain-and-shine coat, grateful that it could bring me in touch with Neil in seconds.

A flashlight cut through the fog. The watchman was peering out. Now he opened the gates for me. I moved slowly inside, signaled my thanks. I couldn't bring myself to ask him to accompany me to the house, as Ferney had instructed.

My hands gripping the wheel overly hard, I wondered about Edouard's whereabouts, half-expecting him to pop out from behind a clump of fog. Was he home yet? Was he waiting for me, somewhere within the shadows of the villa?

As I approached the garage, I instinctively glanced upward. All the windows were dark. The garage door was open. I drove inside. All the cars were lined up except for a green pick-up truck. Edouard must have taken that into town. He wasn't home yet. Relief welled in me.

I cut through the fog-dampened grass to the side door, praying it would not be locked. I reached for the knob. The door was unlocked. I could hear voices in the library. Stephanie and her houseguests, probably reluctant to travel in this weather. They were watching television and drinking. It hardly seemed likely that Edouard—or anyone else—would make an attempt on my life while the others sat down there in the library. They'd probably be there for hours.

Upstairs I locked my door and crossed to the windows to make sure each was locked. I drew the drapes tight against the night. I pulled off my coat, reached for the walkie-talkie, dropped to the edge of the bed. Feeling like a character in a TV drama, I pulled up the antenna, pushed the talk-button.

"Come in," I said shakily. "Come in, please. The weather's fine."

"Glad to hear that." Neil's voice—muffled but recognizable—came to me. "Standing by for possible change in weather. Visibility good." Meaning, he could see the garage. "Check with me in thirty minutes."

"Thirty minutes," I promised, and clicked off, knowing it was wiser not to talk longer than necessary. Still I was disappointed that it was necessary to cut off my vocal contact with Neil.

I went about the routine of preparing for bed, visualizing Neil, sitting off the road in the fog-shrouded Renault only a hundred feet down from the villa gates. The revolver—he'd said it was a snub-nosed .38—was in his jacket pocket.

I turned down my bed, reached for the magazine. I paused before I could pick it up because I heard the unmistakable sound of a car. I hurried across to the window, pulled back a segment of the drapes. The pick-up truck was pulling into the garage.

I hovered there, watching. A figure reached for the overhead door, brought it down to the ground. A few moments later a light shone behind the window shades in the room where I had spied Edouard earlier. He was home. My instinct was to reach for the walkie-talkie and call Neil.

No. Neil must have seen the truck turn in. He'll know Edouard is home. He can see the lights. Wait, Neil. Make sure Edouard stays in his room. *How can he make sure?*

I stood by my window, my eyes fastened to the only pair of lighted windows above the garage, feeling safe as long as they remained lighted because I knew Edouard was inside. Suddenly my throat was tight. The lights in Edouard's room had gone dark. Was he going to sleep— or out into the darkness? Neil was waiting thirty minutes—to make sure Edouard was remaining in his room. *Could he be sure?* my mind taunted.

I sat on the edge of the bed, my hands perspiring from anxiety. Pick up the magazine there on the night table.

Read it. But the words were a blur before my eyes. My eyes moved compulsively to my watch, pushing away the minutes. Listening with every nerve alert to each sound outdoors. Each sound in the corridor.

Outside a twig snapped. I started. A rabbit scurrying through the bushes, I rebuked myself. But I reached for the walkie-talkie with a need to hold it in my hands.

I rose from the bed, walked to the door. Listened to the faint sounds downstairs, seeking comfort. Stephanie and her guests were still in the library. The servants—except for Helene and Frederic, who shared Mme. Simone's wing—were tucked away for the night in the quarters above the garage.

Was Edouard asleep—as I tried to believe—or was he out somewhere in the darkness? Intent on murder? *My murder.* For the dozenth time I consulted my watch. Now. Call Neil now. My finger shook as I pushed the talk-button.

"Weather clear," I reported in response to his acknowledgment. My voice sounded oddly husky.

"I'll stay another twenty minutes. If you don't call, I'll cut out. Okay, baby?"

"Okay."

Edouard must have gone to bed, I rationalized. If he were up to something, I would have known about it by now. And Neil was waiting an additional twenty minutes to be positive nothing was going to happen. *Go to bed, Janice.*

I awoke reluctantly to the sound of a sharp tapping on my door, immediately aware that it was morning. Sunlight seeped through chinks in the draperies. I was astonished that I'd slept straight through the night.

"One moment." I tossed back the covers, reached for my robe. Who was it? What had happened?

"Good morning, Mademoiselle," Helene stolidly greeted me. "Mme. Manet wishes to know if you will join her for breakfast on the terrace. In about twenty minutes?"

"Yes, of course," I stammered. What did Stephanie

want? Had there been another phone call from Paris? But Jacques couldn't call. He had disappeared, with Holly, on a strip of road between that garage and the villa. "In twenty minutes," I promised hastily, because Helene was staring at me.

Inside my room I consulted my watch. I'd slept later than usual. Just this morning when I was so anxious to be back at Ferney's house. Neil must be en route to his *pension* already to collect his morning mail—specifically, the photostat of the marriage certificate which Neil's friend in Rome had managed to acquire. And now I would be delayed over breakfast with Stephanie. What did she want?

I dressed swiftly, a montage of imaginary scenes between Stephanie and me running on a conveyor belt about my mind. Edouard had told her he'd seen me again with Neil—she was about to ask me to leave. She'd had another call, presumably from Jacques—*he* wanted me to leave. Stephanie had decided I was using the villa for a free vacation—there was no missing sister.

Holly and Jacques were married—I couldn't accept the supposition that Holly had married someone masquerading as Jacques, as Stephanie hinted at intervals. Why couldn't the garage mechanic have identified the man with Holly? Then there could be no doubts as all. I was trusting instinct. How much more reassuring to deal with facts!

My eyes focused on the walkie-talkie, still lying on the bed beside the imprint of my body. Don't leave that around. Where could I hide it until I left the villa for Ferney's house? In my shoulder bag.

I thrust the walkie-talkie into the bag. Wishing I dared call Ferney. *No, I mustn't.* How could I know who might pick me up? Had Ferney's men discovered anything last night? I hurt with the lack of knowledge.

Now what should I do with the bag? I can't leave it around. How do I know who might come snooping? In the valise. Hide it in there, lock the valise.

I opened the closet door, pulled out my valise, shoved

the shoulder bag beneath a pair of sweaters. Lock the valise, put it away.

I stood with the key in my hand in fresh indecision. Where did I put this until I was ready to cut out? There was adhesive tape in the bathroom. Tape the key right inside the tiny pocket of my dress. Nobody could possibly see it. Safe there.

Helene had asked me to come down in twenty minutes. It wasn't quite fifteen, but I was impatient. Go on downstairs. Find out what Stephanie wants. Then hurry over to Ferney's house. All through the night his men have been searching. Maybe there's word. I refused to consider that that word might be tragic.

I left my room, headed downstairs. Perhaps Ferney's men know where Holly and Jacques are being held. Perhaps it's only a matter of hours before they can move in and bring them out. By tonight, Ferney said, every inch of ground in the staked-out area will have been covered.

I walked out onto the terrace. Every vestige of last night's fog had vanished. Sunlight laid delicate hands on everything in view. The sky was a glorious blue, the sea passive. The loveliness meaning nothing to me because Holly was missing.

Stephanie had not come down yet. I sat at the table, reached for a French fashion magazine, thumbed through the pages without taking in what I saw.

"Good morning, Janice." Stephanie's voice was brisk, reserved, giving me no inkling as to why I'd been summoned to breakfast with her.

"Good morning." I managed a casual smile.

"I hope I'm not breaking in on your personal plans?"

"No," I denied, my face faintly warm. Did Stephanie mean to be sarcastic? Had Edouard told her about seeing Neil and me last night?

"Janice, I have a special favor to ask of you." Now the impressive Stephanie Manet charm began to surface. "This afternoon and again this evening we have important meetings here at the villa. I would appreciate it if you could arrange to spend the day with my mother." She leaned forward earnestly, her voice low. "You two could lunch at a charming restaurant in Marseille, spend the afternoon sightseeing. Maman adores visiting the cathedrals. For dinner you could stop at a marvelous restaurant halfway between Marseille and the village. I can phone to reserve tables for you for luncheon and dinner."

"It sounds like a lovely day." I heard myself making the anticipated acceptance. *How could I spend the whole day in Marseille?*

"I was sure you'd see me through this crisis," Stephanie purred. "Maman says such awful things sometimes. I never know when she will suddenly go off—" She gestured unhappily. "Edouard will drive you."

"I can drive." I recoiled from the prospect of so much of the day spent in proximity to Edouard.

"Marseille traffic is dreadful," Stephanie explained as Marie came out on the terrace with a carafe of coffee for us. "Let Edouard worry about the driving. I will give him instructions about where you will be dining."

I forced a small smile while Stephanie elaborately described the La Major Cathedral, the Old La Major Cathedral, the Basilica of St. Victor. My mind rebelled at this usurping of the day.

How can I contact Neil? Or Charles Ferney? We've all agreed that, until Holly and Jacques are found, everyone is suspect. Including all the servants. I can't call without fear of someone lifting up an extension in another room. I can't use the walkie-talkie. Neil and Ferney are going to be upset when I don't show this morning.

Marie returned to the terrace with a fluffy herb omelet for me, and a croissant for Stephanie, who was a calorie-watcher. With strained interest I listened to Stephanie, pretended to eat with relish.

"If there is time," Stephanie said, "have Edouard drive you to Pharo Park. From the terrace near the Chateau—where Empress Eugénie once lived—there is a magnificent view of the Vieux Port, the St. John Fort, and La Major—" Suddenly Stephanie froze mid-sentence. "Janice, get down!" She pulled me with her to the meager protection of the heavy pedestal base of the table. "Keep down!"

From a heavy clump of bougainvillea about thirty feet away a bullet whizzed through the morning sunlight. And then another. Stephanie and I huddled together in shock. *Somebody was trying to kill me.* I was staring—mesmerized—into the muzzle of the rifle!

CHAPTER FOURTEEN

"Maman!" Frederic's terrified voice drifted to us from somewhere to the left. "Maman!"

"Frederic, get inside!" I yelled. "Into the villa!"

And then the muzzle of the rifle disappeared. The bougainvillea shook with the impetus of a rapid exit. Shaken, I stumbled to my feet. Stephanie, her face white, rose awkwardly from her haunches. Stephanie had saved my life.

"Somebody had a gun," Frederic stammered, coming into view. "You coulda been killed." His eyes fastened to me. I remember the two glorious red roses on my breakfast tray. Without words Frederic has accepted me as a friend.

"Frederic, he's gone," Stephanie soothed. "It was only a hunter who came too close." But this wasn't the hunting season. And the muzzle of that rifle had been pointed at me. "Go into the villa and find Edouard. Tell him I wish to see him immediately."

Frederic nodded obediently, trotted off with his awkward gait, so incongruous with his impressive physique.

"The villagers are still trying to prevent the sale of the villa," Stephanie said tightly. She thought those shots were meant for her. "It is not enough we have a night watchman. Now the grounds must be patrolled by day as well." She sighed impatiently. "It must wait until Monday—we cannot hire a man today."

"Madame?" Marie peered uneasily from the door to the terrace. "We thought we heard shots."

"You can come out on the terrace now," Stephanie said

155

sharply. "Whoever fired the shots is gone." She touched the carafe. "The coffee is cold, Marie. Bring fresh coffee."

"*Oui*, Madame."

"If you want Edouard to patrol the grounds, I can drive your mother to Marseille," I offered. Remembering Edouard cleaning the rifle out in the garage. Was it Edouard who hid there in the bougainvillea, intent on my murder?

"I just wish him to look around the grounds," Stephanie said impatiently. "Why is it taking Frederic so long to find him?"

"It's only been a moment," I reminded. Was Edouard racing back to the garage to hide the rifle while Frederic sought him in the house?

I don't want to drive with Edouard. But Mme. Simone is my insurance. He won't dare try anything with Mme. Simone sitting right beside me. Will he?

"Stephanie?" Jim Whitney—in swimming trunks and terrycloth robe—sauntered out onto the terrace. "Did I hear rifle shots?"

"A stupid hunter," Stephanie explained.

"This time of year?" He lifted his eyebrows in astonishment.

"The villagers hunt anything on four feet—any time of year. I've warned them about poaching. I must talk to the *sergent de ville*. Was Celia disturbed?"

"When Celia sleeps in the morning," Whitney said dryly, "nothing disturbs her."

"Join us for coffee," Stephanie invited charmingly. Yet I knew she was still unnerved from the encounter with the rifle.

"Thank you, no." His warm smile included me. I sensed a curiosity in him. I'd never exchanged more than greetings with Stephanie's guests except for the night I awoke to the intruder in my room. "I'm intent on a swim this morning."

Stephanie waited until Whitney was out of hearing to speak.

"By Monday all this nonsense will be over. Monday

morning we definitely close on the villa. In a month Whitney's group will take possession. The villagers cannot stop me."

Stephanie was convinced the bullets were meant for her. She'd been too frightened to view the situation logically. In reality, I told myself again, Stephanie had saved my life.

"When would you like us to leave for Marseille?" I asked. If we were not to leave until noon or later, I could drive into the village! There would be time—

"I spoke with Maman already this morning," Stephanie reported. She'd been sure I wouldn't refuse. How could I, in these circumstances? "She would like to leave—" she consulted her watch—"in about thirty minutes. Maman is like a little girl about trips into the city," she said affectionately. "She can have such a delightful time, wandering through the shops along La Canebière, just buying trifles."

"Madame?" Edouard walked onto the terrace. "Frederic said you asked for me." His eyes ignored my presence.

"Before you drive my mother and Mademoiselle into Marseille, I would like you to search the grounds. There were hunters trespassing again." Edouard was new at the villa. He couldn't know if this had happened before. "When you have checked, please bring the Citroën around to the front."

"Oui, Madame."

I fought down an impulse to dash to the garage, to climb behind the wheel of the red compact. I could make it to Ferney's house and back in thirty minutes—but how would I explain such an exodus to Stephanie? I churned with frustration. Why did Stephanie have to decide on this excursion today? But, of course, I knew why. She wished her mother away when the important visitors came out to the villa for the meetings.

Marie brought us coffee. Stephanie's hand was unsteady as she poured for us. A vein throbbed in her temple. I'd never seen her so openly distraught. But Stephanie was convinced the hand behind the rifle meant to kill her.

Stephanie remained on the terrace. I went upstairs for a light coat for the chill of the evening, to collect my shoulder bag. The walkie-talkie was well concealed beneath a handful of tissues. I preferred to take it along with me.

Neil was going to be upset when I didn't show up this morning. How could I get through to him? At the restaurant, when we stopped for luncheon. I'd excuse myself, go search for a phone. In a smart restaurant such as Stephanie would choose there must be a telephone.

I went downstairs. Though it was early, Mme. Simone was waiting for me, jubilant about another excursion into Marseille.

"Oh, I do love the city," she greeted me effervescently. "I'm glad Stephanie forgot to buy a birthday gift yesterday—now we have an excuse to go in again. When my husband was alive, we lived in Paris. That's where Stephanie met Paul. Such a romantic city."

"Edouard's bringing out the Citroën," I said, seeing its sleek whiteness moving along the driveway. "Let's leave now." The sooner we left, the faster I could phone Neil! "We can start out now if you like."

"Yes, let's," Mme. Simone approved with little-girl enthusiasm. "You run out there and tell Edouard not to wander away—we'll leave immediately. I just want to say good-bye to Stephanie."

I went out into the brilliant late morning sunlight, my heart pounding because I couldn't erase from my mind the image of that muzzle pointed at me—and I remembered Edouard cleaning a gun in the garage.

"We will be leaving in a few minutes," I said to Edouard with a formality that was foreign to me. "Mme. Simone will be right here."

"*Oui*, Mademoiselle." He avoided a direct confrontation as he opened the door for me.

Had it been Edouard behind that rifle? My heart was pounding as I sat in the car waiting for Mme. Simone to join me. My instinct was to climb out of the Citroën and run. Yet a stronger instinct held me there. What was the gambling phrase? "Play it as it lays."

Mme. Simone—overdressed for a day in the city—walked to the car with tiny, mincing steps, eyes bright with anticipation as she settled herself beside me.

"It's going to be a lovely day," she promised ebulliently. "We're having dinner at that marvelous seafood place where the lobsters are so delicious you think you're in heaven. I don't care what people say about its being dangerous to eat seafood because of the mercury. I'm going to have lobster for dinner and filet of sole for lunch."

After a battle with Saturday traffic on the autoroute, Edouard deposited Mme. Simone and me before an outwardly modest restaurant, arranging to pick us up two hours later. Inside the lush surroundings we were greeted obsequiously. I gathered that Stephanie was a cherished patron. It was early. Only one other table was occupied.

When we'd ordered our filet of sole amandine, I excused myself to go search for a phone. Mme. Simone was content to sit at the elegantly set table and view the faint trickle of early diners while I presumably retreated to the powder room.

Pointed in the direction of the public telephone, I fumbled in my coin purse for change, not sure what the cost of a call to the village would be, knowing it was late. Knowing that Neil must be anxious at not hearing from me. A chill touched me as I remembered the close call on the terrace this morning. If Stephanie hadn't seen that muzzle aimed directly at me, I might be lying on a slab in a morgue.

Ferney answered the phone.

"Are you all right?" he asked.

"I'm fine now," I said. Faintly breathless. "I was drafted to accompany Mme. Simone to Marseille for the day—" Ferney knew about the scheduled meetings at the villa. He'd mentioned them last night.

"It's Janice," I heard Ferney report, and then Neil's voice came to me. "Jannie, are you okay?" He *was* upset.

"I'm fine, Neil," I insisted. "It's just that I've got hung up for the day. I'm with Mme. Simone in Marseille. Has anything developed?"

"We have the photostat of the marriage certificate and the application. Both signed 'Jacques Manet.' "

"Neil, can we verify the signature?" Not that it was of vital importance when Ferney's crew was in operation, yet I wanted to know.

"Maybe we can. Wait, Jannie."

I hung on, listening to Neil talk with Ferney. And then Neil was back with me.

"Jannie, Ferney is going to ask Odette to check Jacques's signature against documents in the office. She's no handwriting expert," he warned, "but she can make a fairly safe guess."

"Neil—" Should I wait to tell him about the shooting? No, tell him now. I had to share this with him. "Somebody took a shot at me at the villa." How calmly I could say it! Yet my palms were beginning to perspire at the mental recall.

"Tell me what happened," he ordered tersely.

Forcing myself to be calm, I briefed him on the morning's happening. The whole experience seemed so unreal.

"Where was Edouard when it happened?" Neil asked.

"I don't know," I admitted. "He could have been anywhere."

"He could have been behind the gun," Neil said grimly.

"Does Ferney have someone tailing Rochambeau?" He'd said he would.

"Yes, but nothing's come up there. Did Stephanie call the police?"

"No. She's convinced the bullet was meant for her. She's going to hire a watchman for the day. She has no faith in the local police. Neil, she saved my life," I admitted shakily.

"And now you're risking it out driving with Edouard!" Neil shot back. "Jannie, have you flipped out?"

"Nothing's going to happen as long as I'm with Mme. Simone. He won't dare try anything. And we don't know that it was Edouard," I reminded. I refrained from mentioning that I saw him cleaning a rifle. *That* rifle?

"Jannie, I want you to make some kind of excuse. Cut out. Call me. Let me know where you are. I'll come and get you."

"I can't, Neil. I'll buzz you later." Before he could offer more objections, I hung up.

Luncheon was a leisurely affair in the typical French manner. Our filet of sole amandine was an epicurean delight. I refrained from dessert, remembering the lobster dinner. Mme. Simone, with childlike glee, ordered a coffee Bavarian cream.

She was in a nostalgic mood. Her conversation as usual centered around Stephanie. She explained that Stephanie had hired Helene from a jet-set friend who'd decided to sell her villa near Antibes.

"Stephanie knew what a terrible time Helene would have finding a job where they would let her keep Frederic with her. The villagers are terrified of him, you know. Because they don't understand his poor, small, child's brain." Mme. Simone churned momentarily with indignation. "Even Paul was rather upset by Frederic at first. But when Paul was sick—those awful few weeks before he died—Helene helped nurse him. She was a practical nurse, you know, at that mental institution."

"Yes, I realized that." I forced myself to be attentive. My mind was back with Neil and Ferney. How ironic that I must sit here in a chic restaurant with Mme. Simone when the last act of the search for Holly and Jacques was being played out!

Neil must be furious with me for hanging up on him. Yet I can't walk out on Mme. Simone. I have a commitment. Before we leave the restaurant, I must try to call Neil again.

"Janice, it's almost time for Edouard to meet us," Mme. Simone noted with her accustomed emphasis on punctuality. "We'd better go."

We walked out into the broiling afternoon sun of Marseille, to the shrill traffic noises and the zestful parade of pedestrians.

"Oh, I've forgotten my sunglasses!" My ruse to get me back into the restaurant alone. "I'll only be a moment. Stand here under the canopy," I coaxed, drawing her into the shade.

Inside I headed directly for the pay telephone. This time no one answered. Impatiently, fearful that Edouard would arrive and find no place to park in the heavy traffic, I tried again. Perhaps I'd dialed the wrong number the first time. Again, no response. Just the repeated ringing at the other end. Where were Neil and Ferney? What had taken them away from the house?

I hurried out to Mme. Simone. She was waiting serenely for the Citroën, planning her shopping. For the first time since I'd met her she began to speak erratically. For all her show of nonchalance she was obviously upset about the prospective sale of the villa. For twelve years, ever since Stephanie's marriage, she'd had roots here. Even when Stephanie had made the jet-set scene, Mme. Simone had remained at the villa.

"I must buy a small present for Helene," she decided when we were seated in the Citroën en route to her favorite shop. "Whenever I'm terribly nervous, she takes care of me. She knows as much as the doctor. She even gives me my injections."

We shopped interminably, it seemed. I was restless, my mind constantly back-tracking to Neil. The sightseeing and dinner were yet to be endured. Why weren't Neil and Ferney at the house? Had Ferney's men discovered a clue? Had they found Holly and Jacques? I was tense with frustration.

With the shopping completed, we left the Canebière, went down to the Vieux Port, turned on the Quai de Rive-Neuve to the left of the port.

"Did you know," Madame Simone picked up, suddenly vivacious, "that the Phocaeans landed here six hundred years before Christ? The quays were not built until the reigns of Louis XII and Louis XIII." She glowed with

pleasure at being able to impart this information. I suspected that many times she's made the tour circuit to bring
diversion into a poignantly solitary existence. She could
talk to tourists without Stephanie's fearing embarrassment.
"Edouard, take us now to the Corniche Président J.F.
Kennedy," Mme. Simone ordered, slightly imperiously.

In a few minutes we were driving along the Corniche,
running almost its entire length—I guessed about three
miles—along the sea. Mme. Simone pointed out the *Mon-
ument aux Morts d'Orient*—the War Memorial to the Far
Eastern Troops. I admired, to her pleasure, the view of
the islands offshore, and the summit of Mont Marseille-
veyre, which dominates the coast. Somehow I found the
necessary words, though Holly dominated my thoughts.
We were so close to finding her. *So close*. Let her be all
right.

From the Kennedy Corniche we drove onto the Prom-
enade de la Plage, turned left onto an impressively wide
tree-lined avenue. The Avenue du Prado, I noted.

"Edouard, are you taking us to *Notre-Dame de la
Garde*?" Mme. Simone asked coyly.

"*Oui*, Madame."

"I told Stephanie you must see this," Mme. Simone
said with satisfaction. "I can't make the ascent, but I'll
stay in the carport while you climb up for the most magnificent view! On the left you'll see Pomegues and Raton-
neau Island, and off in the distance the Estaque mountain
chain. Straight ahead of you will be St. John Fort and the
Pharo Park. You'll see the port, and to the right the city,
surrounded by hills."

It was a relief when Mme. Simone decided I'd had
enough of sightseeing. The prospect of the lobster dinner
speeded our departure, I suspected, for which I was grateful. In the restaurant I would have a chance to phone Neil
again.

Edouard deposited us at the restaurant, drove off to
have his own dinner. I suggested that he return half an
our earlier than he'd indicated. Mme. Simone was

showing signs of weariness. By the time we'd finished dinner she would be yawning.

The seafood restaurant was situated right at the edge of the Mediterranean, with the splendor of the approaching sunset a fantastic backdrop. A huge, sprawling room, its décor was charmingly nautical. Mme. Simone took herself off to the powder room while I presumably pondered over the menu. When she'd returned and we'd ordered, I went off to commandeer a phone, still uneasy because I'd been unable to reach Neil earlier.

On the second ring the phone was picked up. By Neil.

"I tried to reach you before," I stammered in my rush to communicate. "Where were you?"

"We had a call. Janice, the car was found! The red Ferrari."

"Where?"

"In a barn on a deserted farm six miles northeast of the village. The license plate was removed."

"What about Holly and Jacques?" My throat was dry.

"No trace yet," Neil acknowledged gently. "The men are combing the area. They've got to find them." I sensed rather than heard apprehension in his voice.

"Neil, I'm scared." My voice dropped to a terrified whisper. The car—stripped of its license plate—sat in a barn on a deserted farm. Where were Holly and Jacques? *Were they alive?*

"Baby, you've been great all through this," Neil soothed. "Don't panic now."

"I'm all right." I tried to sound normal.

"Where are you?"

"In a seafood restaurant about halfway between Marseille and the village. Armand's." The red Ferrari was found, and I was about to sit down to a lobster dinner. Hysteria reached out to encircle me. No! Cool, Janice. Play this cool.

"Can you get away from the villa when you return?"

"Nobody can stop me, Neil." These next two hours with Mme. Simone will be a nightmare. To sit at that table and pretend I'm not falling apart with anxiety! "As soon as we get back, I'll take out the car and drive over."

"Jannie, it's going to be okay," Neil insisted with a calmness meant to reassure me. "Hold on, baby."

"I'll be there about nine-thirty, barring accidents," I promised. And shivered. So far, I'd escaped three attempts on my life. How lucky could I be? How lucky were Holly and Jacques?

I returned to our table to find Mme. Simone girlishly pleased at defying Stephanie's orders. She was sipping a martini.

"One cocktail will never hurt me," she insisted. "Why don't you have a drink with me?"

"Thank you, no." I wanted my mind clear.

Paradoxically Mme. Simone embarked on a talking jag about Jacques. Usually it was Stephanie who monopolized her conversation.

"Jacques was only fifteen when I moved into the villa," she recalled sentimentally. "Handsone even then. Always so involved in his chemical experiments. But a marvelous sense of fun, Janice. He adored playing practical jokes." Like bringing home his bride as a surprise? "But never mind," Mme. Simone said archly, "you'll meet him soon." Oh, let me meet him soon! My handsome new brother-in-law.

I made the expected display of enthusiasm for the sumptuous lobster dinner so elegantly served to us. Surreptitiously I consulted my watch at anxious intervals. When Edouard arrived outside with the Citroën, I wanted us to be waiting, not to waste a moment longer than necessary here at the restaurant.

At eight-thirty sharp, with the restaurant jammed to capacity, Mme. Simone and I stood waiting on the simulated ship deck for Edouard to arrive.

"There's the car—" I interrupted Mme. Simone's vocal appreciation of the seascape at dusk. Edouard was punctual.

We settled ourselves on the back seat. Mme. Simone yawned delicately. Before we were a kilometer on our way she was dozing. I sat at stiff attention, my eyes compulsively seeking the speedometer.

Why was Edouard speeding this way? But it was kilometers, not miles, I forced myself to acknowledge. He was permitted to do a hundred twenty kilometers per hour on this road. Nothing can happen to me with Mme. Simone here in the car. Rochambeau would make sure nothing happened to Stephanie's mother. Mme. Simone is my insurance policy.

Edouard cut off onto an unfamiliar side road, detouring around the village, taking a shortcut. Still, inchoate fear raced through me because we were on a strange road. My eyes clung to the passing scenery while I laced and unlaced my hands, as though I must remember every inch of this way.

Because of Holly I stared at every barn, every outbuilding, with suspicion. Had Ferney's crew found Holly and Jacques? They must be somewhere near that deserted farm. *Were they all right?*

When we pulled up before the villa I gently awoke Mme. Simone.

"Oh, dear, was I nodding?" she asked apologetically.

"You had a little nap," I soothed. "I'll walk with you to your rooms."

"I can get there all right," she said, mildly reproachful. "But would you find Helene and send her to me? After two days in Marseille this way, I know I'll need something to make me sleep. Especially after that nap in the car."

"I'll send Helene to you," I promised, chafing under this additional delay. "Would you like her to bring you some hot milk?"

"No. Helene knows what to do," she said, faintly fretful. "Good night, Janice."

I could hear Stephanie and her guests in the seldom-used Louis XIV salon. The tenor of the conversation was apparently convivial. The evening had gone well.

Where would I find Helene? Instinctively I headed for the kitchen. A sulky Marie sat there, slouched over a current edition of the French scandal sheet which Mme. Simone read with the same avidity. Marie, I guessed, was standing by to serve should Stephanie call.

"Marie, do you know where Helene is?" I asked, and Marie jumped as though I'd shouted in her ear.

"In there," Marie said coldly, nodding towards the serving pantry.

Helene was setting silver on a serving tray, laden with delicacies I guessed the visitors from the village rarely enjoyed.

"Mme. Simone would like you to come to her rooms," I reported, startled by the sudden hostility that glowed in Helene's eyes. She resented receiving instructions from me, the intruder. "She's had a hectic day," I added apologetically.

"I will go to her, Mademoiselle." Impassive again. Had I imagined that hostility? "Marie," she called sharply. "Prepare the coffee tray. Then you may serve."

I hastily left the kitchen, hurried down the long corridor to the front entrance, preferring this to the dark, shrub-lined side route to the garage. I took a deep breath as I emerged from the villa into the summer-fragrant outdoors.

Fog was rolling in from the sea again. It was going to be another rotten night for driving. But I must drive to Ferney's house. With time chomping at my back I hurried incautiously down the stairs. Tripped. Fell in an ignominious heap.

For a second I stayed there on my hands and knees. Then, impatiently rising to my feet, I stared hard at something beneath the adjacent kermes-oak shrubbery. Something shiny had captured my attention. At first I thought Celia Whitney had lost a diamond pin.

I reached to retrieve the small round object, squinted at it in the darkness. And then I was ice-cold. Trembling. I recognized the ornate jewel button. *Holly's.*

Before she'd flown to Rome, Holly bought a pantsuit. With characteristic ingenuity she'd decided to replace the unimpressive buttons with ones that were spectacular. I'd gone with her into a favorite button shop specializing in the unusual. She'd bought three buttons like this one.

Holly is here. Somewhere in the villa.

CHAPTER FIFTEEN

I hovered there in the night fog, the button glistening in my hand—the button from Holly's jacket. She'd been so pleased when the clerk brought this one out from the display case. She was here. In the villa.

Call Neil. No time to waste driving to the village in this fog. Helene is with Mme. Simone. Marie is serving in the salon. At this hour Edouard should be in his quarters. Is he? I must take that chance. Use the kitchen phone.

I hurried back into the villa. Moved soundlessly down the corridor to the kitchen. I must alert Neil and Ferney! The kitchen was deserted as I'd anticipated. Voices echoed from the salon while I made the effort to dial with shaking hand.

Neil answered the phone. His voice was crisp, reassuring.

"They're here," I whispered. "Holly and Jacques. Somewhere in the villa. I found a button from Holly's jacket."

I heard the sharp intake of Neil's breath.

"Jannie, you're sure about the button?" Neil the realist.

"Yes! I was with her when she bought the set. They're way out."

"We can't make a move until everybody's gone to bed," Neil cautioned. "Ferney knows the villa. He'll know where to search." Not in the closed-off wing. *Where?*

"Where's Ferney now?"

"He's driving a jeep for one of the teams. When he checks in, I'll brief him. Jannie, you're sure this line is clear?"

"Everybody accounted for," I reassured him. Again, I was working on instinct.

"You stay at the villa. The watchman goes off duty at daybreak?"

"Right." I ached at the prospect of delay. I wanted to run charging through the house, searching for Holly.

"We'll park down the road. When the watchman cuts out, we'll come in. Stay in your room."

"No," I rejected indignantly. "Neil, I've been in on this from the beginning."

"Jannie, it could get rough."

"I'll meet you by the side entrance. I'll see the watchman drive away."

"Wear a swimsuit," Neil ordered. "If you walk into anybody in the villa, explain you're going for an early swim. If you're seen, Jannie, walk away from the villa. Go to the beach. Don't take any chances."

"I won't," I promised. "I'll meet you by the side entrance. Ferney will know where it is. When the watchman leaves."

I hung up just as Marie—apparently startled to find me there—walked into the kitchen. I ignored her sullen stare, smiled defensively, and sauntered off. I recalled no house rule against my using the kitchen phone.

The lively conversation from the salon filtered into the corridor. The local dignitaries were no doubt impressed at being entertained on the grand scale. How late would they stay?

I peered through the picturesque corridor window that gave me a view of Mme. Simone's brilliantly lighted rooms. Sometimes she slept with the lights on all night.

What about Edouard? Where was he? In his room over the garage? Playing cards with Phillips, the Whitneys' chauffeur? Or somewhere in the depths of the villa—with Holly and Jacques? Why did Rochambeau want them held prisoners? Was it Rochambeau, my mind insisted on questioning?

I headed upstairs. At the head of the stairs I halted in shock. Why was the door to my room ajar? I'd closed it.

Who was inside? Brushing away caution, I inched down the corridor. And then I heard the crackling of logs. Realized fires were being started against the night chill. The temperature had skidded sharply in the last hour, which accounted for the fog.

"*Bon soir*, Mademoiselle," Edouard said politely, and I started as he walked through the door. "I have lit the fire."

"Thank you, Edouard." What else was he doing in my room?

I forced myself to walk inside, paused there a moment, with my back to the door. My eyes searched the room, seeking some inkling of impending doom. Nothing.

I locked the door, gazed briefly at the cypress logs crackling in the fireplace, lending a deceptive note of well-being. Still wary, I crossed to the windows to make sure they were locked. Had Edouard noticed, when he'd closed the drapes, that all the windows were locked? What was being plotted now to stop my search for Holly? From where would the next attempt on my life arrive?

How was I going to endure these hours until Neil arrived with Ferney and his men? Knowing Holly and Jacques were in danger. Somewhere in the villa. In the basement? Why had I never thought of that before?

With stubborn determination I changed into slacks and a sweater, kicked off my shoes and slid into sneakers. I couldn't wait until daybreak. The intervening hours were suddenly ominous. *Search now.*

I crossed to a window, pushed aside a sliver of drapes. All the rooms above the garage were lighted. I peered intently, mentally locating Edouard's room. A figure at the window just that moment drew the shade down to the sill.

I made my way downstairs as quietly as I could, conscious of the sounds in the salon where Stephanie was entertaining, praying no one would emerge. Where was the entrance to the basement?

I could not recall ever seeing a door that appeared to lead to the basement. At the foot of the stairs I paused, trying to visualize the kitchen area. It must be somewhere in that vicinity. And suddenly my heart was pounding. I knew the entrance to the basement! That padlocked closet at the far left.

Feeling painfully close to Holly, I sped to the kitchen, ignoring all the warning signals that jogged into position in my brain.

The kitchen was illuminated only by a light above the kitchen range. My eyes closed in on the padlock. Were Holly and Jacques somewhere beyond that lock? How could I get inside? *Who would have the key?* Fresh suspicions whirled about in my brain.

How could I get beyond that lock? Convivial sounds drifted down the corridor, lending me spurious confidence. The servants must have retired for the night—except for Helene, who was with Mme. Simone. How long would Helene be occupied? I must gamble.

I couldn't possibly pick that lock. I didn't know the first thing about such undertakings. Remove one side of the flange. That would open the door. Can I?

I fumbled in a cutlery drawer, came up with a butter knife. Try to remove the two screws. Don't be so clumsy. No, it won't work. The tip's too wide!

I gazed about the room in frenzy, knowing that Holly might be a prisoner on the other side of that door. Where would I find a screwdriver? Search! Search everywhere.

Wildly incautious, I pulled open drawers, searched, agonizingly conscious of the passage of time. How long would Helene stay with Mme. Simone? Would she return to the kitchen this late at night?

Here. A screwdriver. Try it. Why are my hands shaking? Slowly. Work it slowly. I can do it if I don't rush. The bit fits. Turn it a little at a time. There, one screw is out. Remove the other.

Perspiring despite the night chill in the kitchen, I struggled to remove the other screw. Grunted when I dropped the pair of them to the floor. Leaving them there—too impatient to pick them up at this point—I opened the door.

The walls were lined from floor to ceiling with wines and liquors. The room was kept locked against pilferage.

Hastily, I bent to retrieve the screws. Put the flange back into position.

I was thrusting the screwdriver back into its place when I heard footsteps in the corridor. My breath coming in painful gasps, I shoved the drawer closed, reached for the teakettle.

"You wished something, Mademoiselle?" Helene's voice. Sharp. Disapproving.

I swung about, teakettle in hand. My face was hot, heart pounding.

"I was about to make some tea," I stammered. "We had lobster for dinner. I'm terribly thirsty."

"I will bring tea to your room," Helene said formally. "Would you like a pastry with it?"

"Thank you, no. Just tea."

Awkwardly I relinquished the kettle, walked quickly from the kitchen into the corridor. Did Helene believe me? I'd carried it off, hadn't I? She wouldn't notice that I'd tampered with the lock. Would she?

In my room I made a pretense of reading, listening for the sounds of Helene's heavy, sensible shoes. She would probably stay in the vicinity of the kitchen until Stephanie's guests left, I surmised.

I must remain in my room. Wait until Neil showed with Ferney and the crew. We were only hours away from rescuing Holly and Jacques. *I wasn't wrong about that button.*

Helene knocked on my door. I called to her to come in. I'd left the door unlocked in anticipation of her arrival. She brought a pot of tea and a plate of pastries as well. I thanked her self-consciously, waited until I heard her stolid footsteps descending the stairs. Again, I locked the door.

I sat in one of the tapestry-covered armchairs which flanked the fireplace. With the cypress logs crackling, I poured myself tea, made a pretense of debating between the trio of pastries on the hand-painted plate. I ate without tasting, drank automatically because it was something to do. Waiting for daybreak.

The fire was a medley of charcoal and ashes when I changed into a swimsuit. Where was my beach robe, brought along as an all-purpose robe? Make this appear legitimate in the event I encountered someone downstairs.

I pulled the robe from its hanger, drew its comforting warmth about me. In a little while the night watchman would be climbing into his vintage Renault. Neil, Ferney, and his crew would make their way into the villa.

Fighting impatience, I went to a drawer and pulled out the oversized bottle of perfume Holly had sent me from Rome. Wanting small things to do to push away the minutes. In my nervousness I dropped the bottle as I opened it. The exotic, ultra-expensive scent splashed about my sandaled feet.

With a sigh of irritation, I bent to retrieve what remained of the bottle. The carpet would wear this scent for weeks. The perfume stowed away, I crossed to a window, opened the drapes slightly.

The first grey streaks of dawn were brushed across the sky. I strained to see the area before the garage, where the watchman parked his Renault. There he was. Walking to the car. Officially this was daybreak. He was off duty.

I waited, my breathing uneven with anxiety, until I saw the watchman slide behind the wheel of his car, saw the car rolling down the driveway. Neil and Ferney would be watching as he drove through the gates. In minutes they'd leave their cars to creep onto the villa property. Up to the side entrance, as arranged.

As quietly as possible I left my room and tiptoed down the stairs. Halfway down the stairs, I froze. Footsteps below. Who was downstairs at this hour?

Fighting panic, I leaned over the bannister. Frederic, tray in hand, was moving down the corridor. Two exquisite red roses in a slender vase on the tray. I stared at those roses. Those roses were meant for Holly!

I waited till he turned off, at the turn in the corridor that led to the memento room. Then I sped down the remaining stairs.

I can't wait to alert the others—though Neil will be furious with me. I must follow Frederic. Follow the tray that bears two red roses!

My footsteps were silenced by the avenue of small oriental rugs. Trembling, I reached for the knob of the door to the memento room. Opened it, just in time to see Frederic disappear behind a moving panel of wall. The wall on which hung the framed newspaper clippings about the Resistance movement.

The panel closed with a thud. How was I to push it open again? Frenziedly, I ran my hands about the segment which provided entrance. Here! It was beginning to move.

I slid through into a long, narrow corridor. An opening at the opposite end. I could hear Frederic, inside the room beyond, humming softly to himself—a French nursery rhyme.

I bent to remove my sandals, tiptoed down the stone-floored corridor to the opening. In a huge darkened room—its windows boarded up on the outside—sat a strange, barred area, which at first I thought was a cage of some sort. Its only illumination was a forty-watt bulb with pull-chain. And suddenly comprehension clobbered me as I saw the bars, the four bunks sandwiched within the tiny area. This was a re-creation of a cell in a concentration camp, its door now ajar because Frederic was inside.

The food-laden tray with the two red roses sat on the floor. I moved close enough to see the face of the man who lay on the bunk to the left. Asleep. No. *Drugged.* Jacques. As bad as the magazine photo had been, I recognized him.

Frederic straightened up, revealing the occupant of a second bunk. *Holly.* Drugged, I was certain. Her blonde hair fanned about the tiny pillow beneath her head. She was wearing the pantsuit with one button missing from its jacket.

"*Très jolie,*" Frederic murmured, unaware of my presence. "*Très jolie.*"

I hesitated an instant, spun around. Neil. I must find Neil.

"Go inside, Mademoiselle." Helene's almost masculine contralto halted me. My eyes fastened to the gun in her hand. It was pointed at me. One of the weapons from the wall display in the memento room. But I didn't doubt that it worked. "Back into the room," she reiterated, advancing.

"Maman—" Frederic was disconcerted. "Maman, you said you would not hurt them."

"Be quiet, Frederic," Helene shot back. "We connot stop now."

"Helene, why?" I whispered—trying not to stare into the muzzle of that gun.

"You kept looking for them. Why couldn't you go away?" Helene demanded, a vein throbbing in her throat. "Nobody would have to die if you had gone away."

"Maman, no," Frederic pleaded. "You promised."

"Why did you imprison them this way?" Stall. Provide Neil and Ferney with time to enter the villa. Will Ferney know about this? Will they find us? "Why did you drug them?"

"They are drugged to keep them under control," Helene said contemptuously. "A needle in the arm and they are like children. They sleep, they wake, they eat. At my bidding. But you forced your way into the villa!"

"Why are they prisoners?" I demanded. What was she doing? Holding the gun with her right hand, reaching into a black bag on a table at the side with her left hand. My eyes galvanized when I saw her bring out the hypodermic needle. She won't! I'll fight! Where's Neil? Why doesn't he come? "What do you gain from this?"

"Forty thousand francs. To take Frederic to America to the doctors. In America we can disappear. We have false passports. Everything. Monday we leave. Frederic, come over here and hold the gun. She'll just go to sleep, Frederic," she soothed. "Come take the gun."

"Who's giving you forty thousand francs?" I stalled while Frederic reluctantly moved away from Holly, slowly stumbled towards his mother. "Who would do that?"

"The Englishmen. M. Carey and M. Whitney," Helene

said with a triumphant smile. "They know how desperately I need money—for Frederic. For years I have been saving, but it is never enough. They came to me and they told me what must be done. If there are no guests at the villa, Mme. Manet goes every Thursday into Marseille to the beauty salon and to shop. On Fridays she takes her mother to the doctor in Marseille. The Englishmen counted on M. Jacques arriving while Mme. Manet was away. It was easy to dismiss the servants so they would not be in the way. M. Jacques would have stopped the sale of the villa; they would lose a lot of money."

"But how could they know he would arrive on Thursday or Friday?" Keep stalling her! Let Neil and Ferney believe I'd overslept. Let them come searching!

"They had a man following him," Helene said with contempt. "They knew every move he made." She reached to put the gun into Frederic's hand. "Hold it tightly, Frederic. Shoot her if she starts trouble. Remember, it is Maman or her," she exhorted.

Helene advanced towards me with the hypodermic needle poised for injection. I knew I would never awaken if that needle plunged into my arm.

"No!" I moved back into the open door of the cell. Lock myself in the cell with Holly and Jacques. The key's right there! But Helene anticipated my move. She grabbed the key with her free hand.

"You will never know what happened. It will be a peaceful death. For all of you." My eyes dilated with shock. She meant to kill Holly and Jacques as well! "Frederic and I will be far away when they find you."

Helene dropped the key into her pocket, reached for my arm. I stumbled back against the bunk. Fell against Holly.

"Why don't the Englishmen want Jacques here?" Frenziedly I tried for further delay. Rising to my feet I moved back against the wall. Inches from Helene's outstretched hand, which held the lethal needle. "They can buy the villa without his permission. M. Rochambeau has agreed to side with Mme. Manet."

"That is no good now," Helene said tightly. "M. Jacques married. Now the third of the estate which Rochambeau holds in trust for M. Jacques's children passes from his control. M. Jacques makes all decisions. Mme. Manet can do nothing without his approval."

"Maman," Frederic cried piteously as his mother leaned above me, my forearm within her grasp. "Maman, you promised!"

Suddenly a shrill, raucous clanging echoed through the villa, startling the three of us. Helene's hold on my arm involuntarily loosened. Frederic cried out in terror.

"Maman, a fire! It is the alarm! The villa is on fire!"

"No! It is a trick!" But Helene was pale.

I took advantage of that split second of indecision. I kicked Helene sharply in the shin. She bellowed in pain. The needle fell from her grasp and shattered on the floor. As I moved, she lunged towards me. But she was awkward in her massiveness, and I moved with a speed born of desperation.

"Frederic, shoot her!" Helene screamed.

"Maman, no!" His voice followed me as I darted towards the corridor.

"Give me the gun!"

Suddenly the panel at the end of the corridor was opening. Ferney charged into view, Neil at his heels. Neil grabbed me, pinned me against the wall.

Two shots rang out. Helene missed. Ferney did not. Helene, clutching at her arm, fell to the ground.

"Maman, you said nobody would get hurt," Frederic sobbed. "You promised."

"Why did you take such chances?" Neil scolded, holding me close. His face brushed mine. "You might have been killed!"

"She's drugged Holly and Jacques." My eyes moved compulsively to the bunk where Holly lay. "All this time they've been here under sedation."

"They will be all right," Ferney said quietly. "They must sleep off the drugs. That is all."

I pulled away from Neil to reach down to comfort

Frederic. He was sobbing wildly, like a small, terrified child.

"Is she badly hurt?" My voice was overloud. Someone just this moment shut off the fire alarm.

"She will live," Ferney said tersely.

"Frederic, she's going to be all right," I soothed him, while Ferney dropped to his knee to apply an improvised bandage to the flesh wound. "She's going to be all right."

"Paul had this cell built not long after the end of the war," Ferney recalled. "It is an exact replica of a cell we shared at the concentration camp. He built it so that he could never forget those years. When Neil told me about the button you found, I realized then that they were here."

"What's going on?" Stephanie hovered in the doorway. "Why did the fire alarm go off? Why are you all in here?"

"The fire alarm went off because I set it," Ferney said coldly.

Stephanie's eyes found Helene, prone on the floor.

"Mon Dieu! What has happened?"

"Jacques and his wife have been imprisoned here since Friday." Stephanie's eyes found Jacques on the bunk, moved to Holly. I could see her mind grasping this new situation. Jacques was married. He had come home to stop the sale of the villa.

"Helene was under instructions from Carey and Whitney," I said with sudden urgency. "They were paying her forty thousand francs."

"Neil, come!" Ferney leapt to his feet. "Stephanie, call an ambulance for Helene, and Dr. Martine to attend Jacques and his wife. Neil and I will catch up with the Englishmen!"

Charles Ferney, Neil, and I sat at a table on the terrace in the early-morning sunlight, eating the scrambled eggs and sausages that I had prepared, and drinking coffee that was Neil's contribution to our breakfast. I could relax now in the knowledge that Holly and Jacques had been put safely to bed in their rooms. By dinner, according to Dr. Martine's estimate, they would be themselves again.

We had sent the servants, brought to the villa by the sound of the fire alarm, back to their quarters over the garage. To our astonishment it was Edouard who took compassionate charge of Frederic.

Stephanie had gone back to her rooms with the comprehension that the villa would not be sold. Celia Whitney had been given a sedative by Dr. Martine. Jim Whitney and Phil Carey were in police custody.

"Rochambeau had inadvertently mentioned that, until such time as Jacques married, he carried the decisive vote," Ferney summed up briskly. "Up until two weeks ago, Rochambeau refused to side against Jacques, though Stephanie was pressing him. Then Carey, anxious to have the sale tied up because it meant a handsome chunk of cash to Whitney and himself, induced the syndicate to double their offer. Now Rochambeau allowed himself to be persuaded. But at the same time the man hired by them to trail Jacques, to keep tabs on him, reported his marriage. Unless they could seal the deal before Jacques's marriage became public knowledge, the deal was lost. Undoubtedly, they were going to pre-date the contract. They were prepared to stop at nothing—even do away with Jacques and Holly if necessary." Now Ferney checked his watch, pushed back his chair. "For me it is almost time to begin another business day."

"Thank you for saving our lives," I said softly.

"It is enough for me that Jacques has come home," Ferney said with satisfaction. "The son of my old Resistance leader will not forsake his village."

Neil and I walked Ferney to his car, then strolled down the path to the gates, across the public road to the beach, deserted at this hour. Hand in hand we walked along the white sand, enjoying the postcard beauty that sprawled before us.

At the water's edge, Neil pulled me to a halt. Drew me close.

"I know we've known each other a startlingly short

time, so I'll have to allow you a month to grow accustomed to my shortcomings," he said whimsically. "But I absolutely refuse to lose the chance of our honeymooning here at the shore of the Mediterranean. Would you consider early August a likely wedding date?"

"A very likely one," I approved.